Eye of the Predator

by

Matthew J. Pallamary

Mystic Ink Publishing

Mystic Ink Publishing
San Diego, CA
www.mysticinkpublishing.com

ISBN 10: 0692225781 (sc)
ISBN 13: 978-0692225783 (sc)
Printed in the United States of America
San Bernardino, California

This book is printed on acid-free paper made from 30% post-consumer waste recycled material.

Library of Congress Control Number: 2014909736

Book Jacket and Page Design: Matthew J. Pallamary/San Diego CA
Author's Photograph: Matthew J. Pallamary -- Gibbs Photo/Malibu CA

DEDICATION

This book is dedicated to Colleen Kennedy.

CHAPTER ONE

The jungle rushed up to meet Erik as he fell face first into its tangled undergrowth. His breath came ragged, sweat stung his eyes, and his heart thundered in his ears. The sickening sweet rot of decay invaded his lungs, choking him. He held his breath for a moment, listening past the pounding in his ears.

An eerie silence held the forest in its spell.

Struggling to his feet on trembling legs, he heard a low growl behind him. Looking back, he saw two orbs of yellow. For an infinite moment, neither he nor the cat moved, then it crouched and snarled. The hairs on the back of Erik's neck raised in unison with the animal's cry. He could no longer run.

His body went cold, accepting the inevitability of death, then something sparked and new resolve filled him. Hot anger washed cold fear from him and strength returned to his legs. His breath grew low and controlled and his senses peaked, tuned to every nuance of the jaguar's movement. A low growl issued from deep within his own body, his legs bent, and he braced himself for the cat's onslaught.

Man and animal snarled and launched themselves at each other, claws extended, teeth bared, fist meeting fur, flesh meeting fang as Erik and the black jaguar embraced in a savage ballet of death.

The moment languished and Erik had the sensation of floating outside of himself until his awareness shifted and he became one with the cat, sharing its perceptions.

Fully aware, he held on to consciousness, drifting with the jaguar as though tethered like a helium balloon. The world, filtered through the heightened perceptions of his host came to him with a richness and immediacy he had never thought possible.

His surroundings shifted, then came into focus with astounding clarity. Sunshine turned into darkness. Gone were the heavy scents of rotting plants, the palpable humidity, and the riotous jungle growth. The cool night air and rocky terrain he knew from his backpacking trips with Phineas flooded his senses.

The High Sierras.

Together, he and the jaguar loped through pine-scented wilderness sniffing the air in search of prey. Though fully aware of his environment, the cat's instincts enslaved Erik, forcing him to participate in the experience as a passive observer.

Together they moved through the night, stopping every few minutes to listen and sniff before resuming the hunt. A light breeze kicked up, carrying with it smells and sounds. Voices. They moved swiftly through the darkness. Except for nocturnal species too small and too terrified to remain within range of a lethal hunter, their passage went undetected.

The voices came louder. Two of them. And the smells. Stronger. A man and a woman.

"Oh," she moaned. "Honey. Uhh." She sucked in her breath with a hiss. "Feels so good."

The man didn't answer, but his grunts rumbled clear and audible. And the *smell*... Musky. Tangy.

Erik smelled and felt it along with the jaguar and fought to resist, but the beast's excitement drew him helplessly along until they came to a huge boulder overlooking a small clearing.

A moonless, star-filled sky hung over the mountain like a pin-pricked shroud. A small fire had burned down to coals. At the corner of the clearing a tent moved with the sounds and smells of uninhibited sex. The acrid smell of the dying campfire drifted up to them, paling in comparison to the thrill of the carnal scents from the tent.

"Ooh, ooh, ooh." The woman moaned in unison with the man's grunts. The flesh of their bodies slapped together, adding to the rhythm, now frantic.

The cat leaped off the boulder and landed without a sound in the middle of the clearing. Crouching low, it crept toward the tent on its belly. Its hunting lust filled Erik with savage excitement. He knew what was about to happen and wanted to stop, but the overflow of sensory input held him suspended like a fly in the web of a spider.

"Oh, baby," the man said, his voice low and breathless. "It's -- it's coming."

The jaguar paused at the side of the tent.

When the woman's moans turned into a high mewl of pleasure, the cat's ears stood up, then it leaped and snarled, slashing the side of the tent with its claws. Screams filled the night as the jaguar bit and clawed at the tattered, shaking ball of nylon.

Removed, yet part of the scene, Erik witnessed the attack with fascinated horror. Helpless to act, equally helpless to turn away, he felt as though something forced him to witness the carnage. Dying, agonized screams filled him with icy fear while the smell of fresh blood and ebbing life paralyzed him with a lust he had never imagined possible.

Blood soaked through the canvas. Tiny droplets spattered with each swipe of the cat's massive paw. An arm poked through a tear in the tent. The jaguar bit into it and ripped it from its socket. Shredded flesh and bare bone glistened through a gaping hole in the canvas.

The high-pitched screams continued.

Erik groaned and shut his eyes, trying to make the horror go away until his mind filled with bright red and something shook him.

CHAPTER TWO

"Erik!"

His Dad's voice.

"Wake up, you're having another nightmare!"

His eyes snapped open. Twisted sheets pinned his arm to his sweat-soaked body. His heart fluttered and his head hurt. He squinted into bright light and saw the concerned face of his father swim into view.

"You all right?"

Erik took a deep breath and let it out slowly. "Yeah. I'm okay. Thanks for waking me."

"The jaguar again?"

"Yeah, only different. I was closer and I wasn't in the jungle. I was in the Sierras. I watched it find its prey. People. I saw it -- felt it rip them apart. I couldn't do anything."

Phineas leaned forward and ruffled Erik's hair. "It was only a dream."

"It felt like I became the jaguar, but I wasn't. I watched him and I was inside him, but I was outside him at the same time. You know what I mean?"

"I think I do. Dreams can be like that sometimes." Phineas glanced at his watch. "It's time to get up anyway," he said, giving Erik's shoulder a gentle squeeze. "We can talk about this over coffee." He patted him on the back and left the room.

Erik kicked back the covers and noticed tiny spots of blood on the sheets. Looking down, he saw that one of the claws on his amber and claw amulet had scratched him. Clawed by a jaguar, he thought. After all these years. It never scratched me before.

He climbed out of bed and stretched his sinewy body to its full six feet before heading for the bathroom, moving and flowing with a natural grace. Blond hair, intense blue eyes and an angular frame gave him the look of an athletic, Southern California surfer, but what went on behind his eyes told another story.

His early childhood until the time Phineas found him remained a blank; something he had dealt with every day of his life with increasing frustration. His dreams during the last few weeks seemed to take him to the edge of a precipice that separated him from his past, but they always ended abruptly, leaving him alone with his darkness, longing for the truth.

After dressing for work, he went downstairs, made coffee and sat in the study waiting for his father. The large oak paneled room had two walls of books, most of them on zoology and anthropology, many written by Phineas himself. Indian pottery filled the shelves and corners. Spears, blowguns, baskets, ceremonial masks, pipes, and other pieces of native art hung on one wall. A large map of the world covered the remaining wall.

Erik felt more at home here than anywhere else in the house. The artifacts gave him an inexplicable sense of comfort. He often sat for hours studying them with a vague longing, as if one of them might hold the key to his nonexistent past.

"Okay, now?"

His father's baritone, with its Scottish accent broke his reverie. Phineas came in from the kitchen, coffee in hand, looking the part of the distinguished professor, right down to the tweed jacket, wire rimmed glasses, and elbow patches. A wreath of thinning salt and pepper hair crowned his head, but his neatly trimmed beard seemed to make up for the loss above. Thick eyebrows and a prominent forehead accented his probing hazel eyes.

"You've been dreaming a lot more lately," Phineas said, sitting in the wing back chair across from Erik. "Maybe it's time we did some digging." He set his coffee down on the table and leaned forward, forearms on his knees. "Needless to say, I'm as curious as you. You're a gifted and unusual young man."

Erik felt his cheeks flush. "You're the one who deserves the credit."

The old man winked. "You and I both know that you possess some kind of intuitive knowledge that goes beyond book learning. You have a way with animals, boy."

Erik didn't think of himself as gifted or unusual. The credit belonged to his father, who had tutored him. Erik had devoured books almost as fast as Phineas supplied them, quickly catching and passing other kids his age. Naturally, when it came to the choice of careers, Erik followed in his father's footsteps. As a result of Phineas's patient tutoring, Erik had recently received his PhD in biology from the University of California, San Diego, and seemed destined for a brilliant career.

"Whether you like it or not," Phineas continued, "at the rate you're going, I can see you becoming one of the most sought after authorities on animal behavior in the states, maybe even the world."

Erik drained the last of his coffee, then stood and let the empty cup dangle from his finger. "That's the part that bothers me, Dad. I know so much about animals. I can tell you about the life of any animal from gestation to mating to death, but I don't know a damn thing about myself." He shook his head. "It's maddening. You'd think after all these years..."

Phineas rose from his chair and walked into the kitchen with his arm draped over Erik's shoulders. "Tell you what," he said quietly. "I'm sure there's something to these dreams. I've been giving them a lot of thought..."

"Not the shrinks again. I've had enough of those psychoanalyzing Freudian freaks poking at me."

Phineas held up his hand. "An old colleague of mine runs the psychology department at school. He'll talk to you."

Erik shook his head.

"Humor an old man. At least listen to him, if not for yourself, then for me. If you don't like it, you can end it. It can't hurt."

"Dr. Carella?"

Phineas nodded. "Perhaps he'll consent to hypnotizing and regressing you. Your intensified dreams may be a sign that you're remembering."

Erik sighed. "At this point anything's worth a shot."

Phineas patted him on the back. "That's my boy."

CHAPTER THREE

Erik took an elevator to the third floor of the biology building in the Muir College section of the UCSD campus where he and Phineas shared an office on the east side of the building. He walked past labs and bulletin boards, breathing the familiar scents of formaldehyde and alcohol, puzzling over the vividness of his dream. Here in the scientific world with all of its procedures and classifications, life seemed structured and ordered, but when he tried to fathom his own life, the scientific method no longer applied.

He stepped into a corner office at the end of the hall. A partition divided the small area, Phineas working on one side, Erik the other. Animal horns, a tortoise shell, and some bones adorned the top of filing cabinets lining one wall. On another hung a bulletin board peppered with study results, messages, and student reports. Posters detailing animal skeletal structures and nervous systems covered the remaining walls. On his side of the partition, Erik had a PC and printer hooked up to UCSD's supercomputer.

After grabbing a cup of coffee, he logged on and tried to work on a database, but flashes of his nightmare kept him from concentrating. The dream had something to do with his past. He secretly hoped Phineas remembered to talk to Doctor Carella. Maybe the doc had something up his sleeve that would help him remember.

He recognized his father's footsteps coming down the hall. "Good news," Phineas said, coming through the door. "I've just come from the psychology department." He took off his jacket and hung it on a rack by the door. "You have an appointment with Doctor Carella this afternoon at two."

Erik felt as if a weight lifted from his shoulders. "That's great..." He stopped. "Oh no, I just remembered…"

"Don't worry about it. I'll teach the class for you."

"Thanks."

He left his office at quarter to two that afternoon and headed for the psychology building. While walking across campus he thought of his teen years and all the time spent with psychiatrists trying to unravel his blank past. To date no one had succeeded. It felt like he had not existed for the first half of his life. After countless psychotherapy sessions, hypnosis, and past life regressions that he didn't believe in, he and Phineas finally gave up in frustration.

Now his dreams came stronger, with greater immediacy. Maybe the time had come. He dreamed of being chased by jaguars for years, but none of them had been as lucid and surreal as this last nightmare. Its vividness made the undercurrents of his mind shift and swirl like silt in the bottom of a stream. He sensed something about to break loose and dreaded what he might discover, but anything was better than not knowing.

He found himself looking up at the psychology building, a small three story structure connected to the linguistics department. The directory had two Carellas listed as clinical researchers. Nicholas and Nicole on the second floor, Room **2050**.

His father said that Dr. Carella worked with his daughter. Erik hadn't realized she was a professor. He shrugged. She probably wore coke-bottle bottom glasses and looked like an entomology specimen.

After hustling up the stairs, he found the office, put his hand on the doorknob and froze. Apprehension gripped him and his thoughts took flight like birds. He took a long breath and let it out.

Nothing's going to happen he told himself, trying to push past his apprehension. "Hell with it," he muttered. "Too many years of not knowing. I'm too damned close to chicken out."

His sweaty hand slipped on the knob as he twisted, then the door swung open. He stepped inside, aware of the thumping of his heart.

The tiny outer office had two uncomfortable looking plastic chairs against one wall alongside a small table full of magazines. Though the walls had the same dull gray cement of most of UCSD's buildings, these came to life with oil paintings of pastel colored flowers and a scene he recognized as La Jolla cove at dusk; rose colored with tiny lights winking on the horizon and white crested breakers crashing on the shore.

"Dad painted those."

He jumped at the feminine voice and spun around to see a beautiful woman with long, silken black hair, soft brown eyes, and a small, delicate nose accented by high cheekbones and full lips.

"Sorry. I didn't mean to sneak up on you like that." Her warm, velvety voice put him at ease. She wore a gold watch and necklace, a powder blue blazer, and a matching skirt. Her frilly white blouse had the top button open, an image that seemed both sexy and conservative.

Erik caught himself gawking. "Um... Hi. I'm... I'm Erik, Erik Simpson. I had a two o'clock appointment with Doctor Carella."

She glanced at her watch. "You're right on time."

"You're Nicole?"

She looked down at herself. "Last time I checked."

Put your tongue back in your mouth, he thought. "My Dad's a good friend of your father."

She held out her hand. Erik took it, catching a whiff of her perfume. She gave his hand a gentle squeeze that melted his fear.

"Dad's tied up with some last minute grant paperwork. If you don't mind, I'll be working with you."

"Well, um, actually I was expecting your father."

"I'm the next best thing."

"I'm sure you are."

She crossed her arms. "You're uneasy because I'm a woman, right?"

"Nothing personal, but -- well, I'd feel better talking to a man."

"Please, come into the office," she said. "Have a seat. Relax."

She turned and he followed her lingering scent, unable to keep his eyes from the curve of her hips and the shape of her calves. He felt guilty looking at her this way, but he couldn't stop himself. Every part of her seemed right.

Larger than the outer room, the inner office had more paintings done in the same colors and bold strokes that made them jump out from the lackluster gray wall. Psychology books lined a second wall. The third had prints of travel posters from Paris, Rio de Janeiro, and Vienna, and in the fourth, windows that looked out over the campus. A vase of fresh cut flowers adorned a small table in the corner. She closed the door and motioned toward a chair, then sat behind the desk.

Erik found himself looking for a ring, wondering if she had any romantic involvements. No ring.

When he glanced up, her gaze locked on his. "Tell me about yourself."

"Like what?"

"Some background. Why you're here."

"Didn't my Dad?"

"I want to hear it from you. You live with your father, right?"

He felt embarrassed about not living on his own. "We share a two-story house in La Jolla. Eighteen years ago he found me unconscious during an expedition in South America. A week after he adopted me his wife died."

"Sorry to hear that."

"Drunk driver."

Empathy flickered briefly in her eyes, but she said nothing.

"He spent all his time raising and teaching me," Erik said, hurrying the words along to spare her from discomfort. "He did a hell of a job too. He swears I have an understanding of animals and life processes that goes way beyond anyone he's ever met."

"Why do you think he says that?" She ventured. "I mean, what do you think?"

He sighed. "At the risk of sounding egotistical, I can feel it," he said, sure of himself, yet unable to find the words to express it. "It's a knowing." He tapped his chest with his finger. "Inside of me."

She leaned back in her chair, crossed her arms and studied him. "Would you call it insight?"

"Intuition," he answered without hesitation. "I can feel their inner lives as if what's missing in mine is made up for in what I know of theirs. Like the way a blind man's other senses grow sharper with the loss of the one…" He stopped, feeling he had said too much.

An awkward silence hung between them, Erik not volunteering more, Nicole not pushing. Her brow furrowed, then her features softened. She leaned forward, her soft brown eyes questioning. "Can you trust me to try and help you find what's missing?" she whispered.

Erik felt a swell of emotion. In that moment he wanted to abandon himself to her like a child loving its mother.

"I have to know," he said evenly. "The whole first half of my life is a blank. I don't remember a thing. Now the dreams are getting more real. They're part of it. I know…"

"You have an unusual case of amnesia," she said nodding slowly. "It's uncommon to have a complete erasure of your past, particularly for such a long period of time. Uncovering whatever's buried may not be pleasant."

"I know, but all these years of not knowing. I can't take it anymore. I have to know."

"I think you've come to the point where you're strong enough to deal with it. Have you ever been hypnotized?"

"I never seem to go under."

"Are you willing to try again?"

"I never felt comfortable with the other doctors. I don't trust them."

A smile played across her full lips.

"I think that's enough for now," she said, rising abruptly.

Erik didn't want it to end.

"Let me talk this over with my Dad," she said. "Then I'd like to try hypnosis." She handed him a business card. The address was on Mango Drive in Del Mar. "Can you make it tomorrow afternoon, say at four?"

He tucked the card into his pocket. "Sure."

"We'll see if we can uncover whatever's below the surface of this trauma. Amnesia is usually short term. There's something more here. If we get to what's holding you back, it could be overwhelming. You sure you're prepared to deal with it?"

Erik looked up at her, gaze steady. "Are you?"

CHAPTER FOUR

Erik studied the tangle of undergrowth where he had fallen. His heart pounded his ribs and his breath came short and hard. The heaviness of the jungle's humid air pressed on his chest.

Thin shafts of sunlight pierced the dense canopy above, streaming down through heavy mists, diffusing their light to shadows of silver and gray. Huge ferns hung low, bowed in silent witness to their oppressive surroundings. A bright green insect fanned its wings in front of him, watched by the single unblinking eye of a lizard until the predator's tongue lashed out in a blur of movement. Erik shuddered, knowing how it felt to be the prey.

The thought of staying where he fell flitted through his mind with the tenuous hope that his pursuer might pass him by, but he knew better.

The jaguar was a skilled hunter.

Even now it stalked him, creeping silently, ready to pounce.

He pushed a clump of long blond hair away from his sweaty forehead and tried to remember how he came to be the prey. A haze clouded his thoughts as though the dense, early morning mist had seeped into his mind, obscuring his memory. He didn't know where he was, who he was, or where he came from. He knew only fear and the instinct to survive.

The mournful cry of a jungle bird jolted him. Sensing the nearness of his pursuer, he rose and stumbled through the dense undergrowth. Dizziness washed through him and vines whipped his face. Startled birds flew from their nests. He slipped on a rock and fell again at the base of a tree.

A large python slithered toward him from above. He crawled, then stood on wobbly legs and wiped stinging sweat from his eyes. Looking down, he saw blood smeared with sweat on his hands, then the amulet around his neck. Amber with two teeth and two claws. What did it mean? Another rush of dizziness swayed him. He tried hard to think.

He spotted an orange glow at the same moment he sensed predatory eyes behind him. A shiver coursed down his spine, then wracked his whole body. His head inched slowly in the direction of the jungle behind him, freezing when his eyes locked with the gaze of a black jaguar.

Close to seven feet long with short, massive limbs and a large head, the cat bared its fangs, hissed and crouched lower, preparing to leap.

Erik braced himself for the inevitable frenzy of claws and fangs, then turned back toward the orange glow. Fire. Men. Could he reach them? Probably not, but better to die trying.

His own savage animal scream erupted from inside him as he bolted toward the orange. He heard the jaguar close behind, cutting the distance quickly. He imagined claws raking his back, hot animal breath on his neck and teeth sinking into his flesh as they found the base of his skull, cracking his spine like a twig.

The cat snarled and leaped. Its shadow hovered, blocking out the forest for an eternal moment before hitting with an explosive crack that drove him forward under its weight. A bright flash filled him.

Erik sat up straight in bed, heart dancing to a staccato beat, chest tight with fear. Sweat soaked his body.

The dream. Third time this month. Same dream.

He glanced at the digital clock on the nightstand. *Eleven-thirty*. Might as well get up. He wouldn't be able to sleep for awhile now. Not after the dream.

He went downstairs and sat in the study, trying to sort out his thoughts and emotions. Phineas appeared in the doorway a few minutes later in slippers and a red flannel bathrobe.

"Private party or can anyone join?"

"Couldn't sleep."

Phineas dropped into a chair across from him. "Another dream?"

"Feels like I'm on the verge of something. Can you tell me the story again?"

Phineas settled back, crossed his legs and studied his son. "You think it might help?"

"It's been awhile since you told it."

Phineas hesitated, as if collecting his thoughts, then launched into a monologue as though addressing a class. "It was a joint zoological expedition for UCSD and the zoo in the Darien Gap; two hundred and fifty roadless miles of rain forest that separate Colombia from Panama. Probably ten or twelve miles east of a Tukano village."

Erik studied the wall map and focused on the part of South America his father described.

"It was early morning and the sun had only been up a short while. We were cooking breakfast when I heard the most ungodly shriek." Phineas's eyes took on a faraway look.

"I grabbed my rifle and there you came, running out of the jungle, screaming like a banshee, looking wilder than any animal I'd ever seen. I'll never forget the expression on your face." He shook his head.

Even now, the memory still covered Erik with goose bumps.

"I started to put my rifle down when I saw the jag. All black. Surprised the hell out of me. I had never heard of one going after someone so close to a camp full of people. Something had to be wrong with it." His voice dropped and he continued, seemingly more to himself than to Erik. "Its behavior was totally out of character."

Phineas looked up and his eyes came back into focus. "Its front paws were inches from your heels. I had to act quickly or you were a goner, but he was so close I feared hitting you. I figured you were dead anyway, so I took the shot just as it leaped. The two of you went down. I wasn't sure I hit it until it went limp. I felt bad about killing the beast, but I had no choice."

"You never like to see anything killed," Erik mused. "Not even bugs."

His father smiled wistfully. "It was a beautiful specimen." He shook his head. "Such a waste. Anyway, I thought you were both dead until I rolled the jag away and saw you unconscious but breathing. A sorry sight if I ever saw one. A white boy, maybe ten years old, wearing nothing but an Indian loin cloth and your jaguar tooth and claw amulet. Your body was painted like a Tukano shaman and your hair was a rat's nest. I brought you into camp, cleaned you up and watched over you 'til you regained consciousness."

"Other than my dream, that's the first moment I've been able to remember, even after all these years," Erik said.

"That's been your birthday for eighteen years now."

"As far as I know, my life began the second I woke up and saw you leaning over me."

"Until you started having these dreams."

"It's the only glimpse I've had from the time before you found me."

Phineas nodded. "Looks like your meeting with Nicholas's daughter might've stirred something up."

Erik smiled. "Got to be honest with you, Dad. Meeting her stirred up a few somethings."

Phineas arched his eyebrows. "Oh?"

"You ever see her?"

"No, but I spoke to her on the phone. Sounds like a charming young lady."

"How 'bout gorgeous."

"Don't set yourself up for a disappointment. She's a psychologist. Getting involved with subjects is taboo."

"But not unheard of."

"Even if she were attracted, I don't think she'd get involved. She's very serious about her research."

"You always told me to keep an open mind."

Phineas smiled and stood. "I'm going to go get a cup of hot chocolate. Care to join me?"

"Why not?" Erik followed him into the kitchen. Talking things over had settled his mind. Nobody knew him better and nobody meant as much to him as Phineas. At times like this he felt his deepest love and respect for him.

In spite of his father's warning, Erik couldn't wait to see Nicole again. He would respect her wishes if she wanted to keep her distance, but his feelings toward her were strong.

When he finally went to bed, it wasn't the swelling of emotion for his Dad that kept him from sleep and it wasn't his preoccupation with his problems, or his nightmares.

Nicole filled his thoughts.

CHAPTER FIVE

Phineas and Erik had a set of offices at the San Diego Zoo where they oversaw research and ensured that the animals were kept healthy. While flamingos greeted visitors at the front gate and double-decker buses carried tourists and excited children around the grounds, Phineas and Erik worked on the top floor of an unmarked two story wooden building overlooking a long single-story stuccoed complex that served as an animal holding quarters in the southeast corner of the zoo, behind the Wegeforth Bowl.

Downstairs, they had a fully equipped treatment room and a console filled with television screens that monitored the animals in the complex. Although Phineas and Erik were competent veterinarians, they relegated major surgery to their colleague, Dr. Hoffelder.

The complex had a quarantine area for new arrivals and an observation section for animals recovering from sickness or surgery. More often than not the cages held animals on loan from other zoos and animals being prepared for loans from the San Diego Zoo.

Phineas had an antique roll top desk overflowing with papers. His working light came from an old green banker's lamp. On top of a worn blotter sat a laptop computer and a jumble of pens and pencils sticking out of a mason jar. Diagrams of reproductive cycles and genetic structures covered the walls of Phineas's domain, computer flow charts and directories to databases covered Erik's.

After spending the morning recounting Erik's "birth", the two sat working at their respective desks. Erik filled in the last lines of a grant proposal and leaned back from the screen, rubbing his eyes. "Feel like Mexican, Dad? I was thinking we could stop for lunch at El Indio's on the way to UCSD."

"Sounds good. We can sit outside."

"All right. I'll let you…" Erik's heart swelled with what felt like great emotion. He'd felt this way before, but never this strong. Physical and emotional, connecting his heart and mind.

"Let me what?" Phineas called back.

"Something's wrong with that tiger that came in yesterday."

"What the devil are you talking about?"

"A feeling. Something's wrong."

"Oh, *that* feeling."

Erik heard the chair pushing away from his father's desk, then Phineas poked his head around the partition. "Well, then we'd better go take a look, hadn't we?"

They rushed downstairs and did a quick scan of the bank of displays. On monitor six a Bengal Tiger rolled on the floor of its cage, writhing and hissing.

"Quickly!" Phineas said.

His father's voice came from far away. Bizarre emotional impressions bombarded his mind. Pain blossomed at the base of his skull.

"Quickly!" Phineas said again, jolting him back to the moment. "Grab the noose and a tranq gun."

Erik ran to the storeroom, grabbed the noose and gun from the wall and ran after his father. The agonized roars of the tiger came to him through the door when Phineas opened it. Erik hustled in behind him, breathing in the familiar, musky animal smells.

Chattering, birdcalls, howls, and other sounds of animal panic filled the building until Erik came through the door. The moment he entered, the noises ceased. The eerie silence sent a chill dancing down his spine, until he heard the growl of the big cat. As he neared the cage, the pain at the base of his skull increased. The tiger rolled around on its back, jaws clenched in an agonized vocalization that fell somewhere between a roar and a hiss.

"It's pressing on his brain," Erik said. "I think it's a tumor. We'd better tranq him."

Phineas looked sideways at his son, then took the gun and leveled it at the writhing tiger.

The big cat pawed the air. Flecks of foam flew from its muzzle as it thrashed from side to side and its tail beat the ground.

Erik rubbed the back of his head. "We don't have a lot of time."

Phineas studied his son a moment longer. "You haven't been wrong yet." He squeezed off a shot. The dart found its mark in the cat's flank. The tiger bellowed, rolled onto its side and tried to pull itself forward, dragging lifeless rear legs behind.

"It's at the base of his skull," Erik said through the pain. "I can feel it pressing against the nerves of his spine."

The cat pulled itself along for another step or two, then stopped and studied them with glazed eyes before its head lolled to the side and went limp.

Freed from the pain, Erik started for their offices, calling over his shoulder as he left. "I'll get hold of Dr. Hoffelder and bring the gurney so we can get the cat prepped."

He heard his father unlocking the cage door as he went out.

The smell of disinfectant and alcohol filled the air where Erik held two flaps of loose, shaved skin on the tiger's neck together under the bright lights of their operating room. Phineas monitored the cat's vital signs and anesthesia as Dr. Hoffelder put in the last few stitches. A baseball-sized tumor lay in a stainless steel tray on a cart littered with bloodied instruments. Hoffelder applied a bandage and gave the tiger another shot in the flank.

"That ought to keep him settled for awhile." The doctor removed his cap, gloves, and mask, revealing bushy eyebrows, and a bulbous nose. Though short and heavy, his hands were thin and nimble. "Keep him on IV's and give him a shot every six hours," Hoffelder said with a German accent. "I'll be back to check on him in a few days." He wiped a film of sweat from his forehead.

Erik and Phineas removed their surgical gowns and followed the doctor out of the operating room into their outer office.

Phineas made a beeline for the coffee maker. "Coffee Fritz?"

"That would be nice. It got a little touchy in there."

Phineas nodded. "Six hours."

Erik rolled a chair from behind a desk, sat backward on it and faced the two older men.

"How the hell did you diagnose it so quick?" Hoffelder said. "I know you two are good, but you don't have equipment that could give an accurate diagnosis, especially in such a short time. I don't have to tell you, if it hadn't been found so quickly, we would have lost a very expensive animal."

Erik and Phineas exchanged glances, but neither spoke. No one would take Erik's impressions of the animal's pain seriously. Even he had a hard time rationalizing it, yet he knew with absolute certainty what the tiger's problem had been. How could he explain that?

Phineas spoke up, rescuing him. "Erik and I found him writhing on the floor, trying to rub the back of his neck. We knew something wasn't right. I'd seen similar behavior in a cat years ago, so I tranqued him and had Erik call you. In that case it turned out to be a tumor, just like this one."

"Do you know what the chances are of that happening twice?"

"I couldn't believe it myself."

Hoffelder looked from Erik to Phineas, then shrugged. "You are the experts."

After the doctor left, Erik sat with his father in silence, until Phineas spoke. "That was the damnedest thing, son. I don't know how you did it."

"I don't know either, Dad. All I can say is I felt it and *knew* it."

Phineas leaned back in his chair and steepled his fingers. "You don't suppose it has anything to do with the dream, do you?"

CHAPTER SIX

Erik looked up at the sky as he drove north on I-5. The thick marine layer shrouding the pale sun reminded him of the misty wall obscuring his past. He couldn't wait to talk to Nicole again. Maybe she could help him break through his own overcast mind the way the sun broke through San Diego's June gloom to bring light and warmth to his beaches. The darkness of his past had cast a pall over his every waking moment for too long now.

His experience with the tiger left a frantic jumble of thoughts and images spinning through his mind. Part of him dug voraciously in search of buried knowledge while another part blocked his thinking, as if protecting him from something forbidden.

He took the Del Mar Heights exit and drove a few blocks toward the ocean before pulling into the parking lot of a two-story wooden frame building where the Carellas had a suite of offices on the second floor.

Oil paintings and bright tapestries hung on paneled walls and blue plush carpet covered the floor of the reception area. Inside Nicole's office rows of books lined the walls and a silk flower arrangement sat in a large brass urn in one corner. A vase of fresh cut flowers adorned her desk.

Erik took a seat across from Nicole and breathed in slow, trying to calm himself. "Nice office."

In contrast to how he felt, she looked relaxed and professional in tan slacks and a suede jacket. "I spend a lot of time here," she said. "So

I've taken pains to make it comfortable." A hint of her perfume caressed him, working its magic on his troubled thoughts.

Erik opened his mouth thinking he was going to ask her for a date, but found himself talking about the tiger. "I'm sure my Dad told you about my rapport with animals."

"As a matter of fact, he did."

"It's turned into something a little more complicated than simple rapport."

Her eyebrows raised. She leaned back in her chair. "Tell me about it."

Erik told her about his experience with the tiger, including the physical pain he felt and the stunning accuracy of his diagnosis. As he relived the experience, he caught himself rubbing his neck at the remembered pain.

When he finished, Nicole remained lost in thought, staring out her office window. Erik kept silent, thinking that she didn't believe him, wondering what she would say or do. Eventually, she turned her gaze on him, her soft brown eyes full of questions.

"I've talked this over with my father," she said. "He agrees that hypnosis is the best approach. What do you think?"

"At this point I'm willing to try anything. Hypnosis didn't work in the past, but I think these dreams are telling me something."

"Then let's give it a whirl."

Erik felt a stab of panic. "Now?"

She stood and gestured toward a leather recliner. "Now's as good as ever. Lie back and get comfortable. Relax."

Erik slid onto the recliner, feeling tense. Nicole went to a door built into the wall and opened it. A moment later, the soft, comforting sound of ocean waves rolling onto the beach filled the office, then the lights dimmed.

She took the high-backed chair from behind her desk, rolled it over and sat next to him. "Take a deep breath," she said. "And let it out slowly. Allow yourself to relax."

Erik did as she said. Now that she was closer, her perfume tantalized him. God, what he would do to get even closer.

"If we're successful, I'm going to persuade you to hypnotize yourself. I'm hoping that my suggestions will relax you enough to put you into a trance. There's no big mystery to it. If you're not comfortable and you're not cooperative, it won't work. If you can trust me, you'll put yourself under. Are you ready?"

He nodded.

She pulled a penlight from her pocket. "Watch the light," she said softly. Holding it in front of him, she moved it back and forth. "Listen closely to my voice."

Swinging the penlight back and forth, she continued, her voice even and authoritative. "Keep your eyes on the light and listen to my voice."

Erik listened, feeling silly, then he remembered what she said about hypnotizing himself, so he put his concentration into what she told him.

"That's right." Her silken voice dropped, sounding still smoother. "Follow the light with your eyes. You'll find that as you follow it, your eyes are getting tired. That's okay. Watch it swing back and forth. Back and forth. Follow it with your eyes. They are growing tired. Feeling heavy. They want to close. Rest. Back and forth. Back and forth. They *are* getting heavier, aren't they?"

Erik became aware of the weight of his eyelids. He struggled to keep them open, feeling the importance of watching the light.

"Don't fight it," she said softly. "Just follow. Back and forth. Your eyelids are getting heavy. Heavier. You can barely keep them open."

His eyelids took on more weight with each word. He gave up fighting, closed his eyes, and resolved to simply listen to her voice.

"You're drifting. Drifting down. Gently. Drifting. Down into your mind."

He listened to her soft whisper lulling him as he faded and slipped into a dreamlike state, listening, letting her voice guide him.

"You're drifting further *down* into a feathery sleep. It's light and refreshing, drawing you deeper, *deeper*, more restful. Down into your mind. *Deeper.*"

Erik floated down, pulled by the gentle insistence of her voice.

His face felt wet when he opened his eyes to find Nicole studying him with a puzzled expression. The music had ended. Beside her lay a note pad and a voice recorder that hadn't been there before.

"Sorry. Looks like I fell asleep," he said, feeling embarrassed for her.

"You've been under for close to an hour," she said.

"An hour?" His heart jumped. "What did I say? Did you learn anything? Do you know where I came from? Who I really am?"

"Well..." She struggled for words. "I'm not -- I don't -- I'm not sure what to say."

"What do you mean?"

"I've never seen or heard anything like this before." She hit a button on the recorder. "The strangest thing. I managed to regress you and I heard all about your teenage years with Phineas, how he raised you, taught you manners, hygiene. I even got back as far as the day he found you in the jungle." She hugged herself as if she had been the one chased by the jaguar. "You told me what it was like being hunted. I saw the terror in your eyes."

Erik's impatience welled up. "And?"

"You wouldn't go any further. Like you ran into a mental wall." She paused as if grasping for the right words. "More like a mental haze. You were so afraid. I coaxed you. Tried to get you to face the fear, but you withdrew, curled up in a fetal position, and started sobbing. When I tried to calm you, your sobs grew heavier. Then they weren't sobs anymore." Her voice trailed off.

"If they weren't sobs," he said, unable to contain his impatience, "what were they?"

"The most authentic imitations of animal calls I've ever heard."

Her words punched into him like broken glass. "What?"

"And you acted out the part of each one."

Confusion filled him. "I what?"

"Listen." She hit the play button.

Erik heard himself chirp like a bird, chatter like a monkey, growl like a tiger, then cry like an eagle. After a pause, he heard a wide repertoire of animal sounds, each sounding surprisingly real. Each new sound jolted him more than the preceding one. At first he thought she might be playing a prank, but her expression told him different.

He stared at the recorder, not knowing how to respond. "That's me?"

"I couldn't believe it," she said. "As you went through the bird calls you craned your neck and opened your mouth as if waiting to be fed. When you mimicked the tiger, you got up on all fours and moved your head from side to side while growling. I almost brought you out of it at that point, but you continued responding to my voice, so I talked you through it."

A wave of nausea washed through him. His shirt felt soaked with sweat and his skin felt prickly. A dull headache throbbed in the back of his head, building like a storm front. "Shut it off!"

Nicole hit the stop button.

His mind spun in the sudden silence filling the office. Nothing made sense.

"Relax," she said calmly. "Tell me what you're thinking."

"I -- I don't know -- I'm scared." He gripped the arms of the chair with shaking hands and squeezed until his knuckles turned white. Tears streamed down his cheeks. He felt humiliated without knowing why. The worst part was that he didn't know any more than he had before coming.

She came to his side, sat on the arm of the chair and rested her hand on his shoulder. "It's okay," she said. "It'll hurt until you work through it, but you'll get past it."

Erik felt something let loose inside him and he began to sob. "What's wrong with me?" he said. "Am I crazy?"

CHAPTER SEVEN

E rik drove home in the rain, his thoughts a torrent of hidden fears. Hearing himself mimicking animals had driven his foreboding to the surface, yet he still had no inkling of his past.

He walked into the house unable to eat, work, or read. He turned on the television to distract himself, but its mindless chatter only added to his confusion. He wanted to discuss his feelings with his father, but he didn't know how to voice them. Instead, he went upstairs to bed, hoping he could escape into sleep.

Hands behind his head, he closed his eyes and listened to the rain hammering his window, thinking about the way Nicole dealt with him. Recalling her gentle touch and the sweetness of her perfume brought a faint smile before he slipped back into emotional chaos.

After Phineas came in, the house settled into silence. Erik lay awake in the darkness, finally drifting off into a troubled sleep some time after two.

The following morning he went to the holding complex to check on the recovering tiger.

"How you doing, boy?" he asked as he let himself into the cage.

The drugged cat lay on its side, eyes open, but glazed, its ribs rising and falling with the slow rhythm of its breathing. The tiny pink tip of its tongue hung out of the corner of its mouth.

"Hope you're feeling better today." Erik stroked the cat behind its ear. "Don't worry, I'm only checking to make sure you're healing all right."

He put a fresh dressing on the wound and replenished the IV.

"That'll take care of you for now." He patted the tiger's flank, then put his supplies back in his bag. Before leaving he knelt in front of the tiger, studied its glossy eyes, and wondered what had gone on in its mind when he had sensed its pain.

"Believe me," Erik said. "I know what you were going through." He rubbed the back of his neck. "What happened with us? Did you tell me? Did I pick up on it?"

The cat made no response.

Erik shrugged. "I guess if you knew, you couldn't tell me anyway, could you?" He stood and stroked the cat's head. "Well, buddy, if anything bothers you, just give a growl. I'll be keeping an eye on you." He nodded toward the camera that monitored the cage.

He heard the clicks and clacks of his father's keyboard as he went up the stairs to their offices.

"How's the cat?" Phineas asked without looking up.

"Seems to be doing fine. I changed his dressing and gave him a new IV. I'll check on him again before lunch."

"How are *you* feeling this morning?"

He thought about his session with Nicole and how little sleep he had gotten, but decided not to burden his father with it. He needed time to think. "I didn't have any nightmares."

"Good. Nicole Carella called this morning. She sounded concerned."

"Everything's cool." Anxious to put his problems out of his mind, Erik buried himself in his work, stopping only to listen to the comforting rat-a-tat of his father's typing. He lost track of time until the phone rang, jolting him. He snatched it up. "Hello?"

"Hi, this is Lieutenant Mitchell with the U.S. Forestry Service. Could I please speak to Erik or Phineas Simpson?"

"This is Erik."

"You were referred to me by the U.S. Zoological Society. They say you're the best." He paused. "We have an unusual animal problem up here at Big Pine."

"Big Pine?" Erik felt cold in the pit of his stomach. "I know the area. My Dad and I backpack up there. What's the problem?"

"A bizarre animal attack. In fifteen years in the forestry service, I've never seen anything like it."

The sensation in Erik's stomach deepened.

"Some time in the past couple of days two people were fatally mauled by a large animal. We're having a problem identifying it. Whatever it is, it's not indigenous to this area. I was hoping you could fly up here this afternoon and give us a hand."

"This afternoon?"

"There's a chopper on standby. It can pick you up at Lindbergh in a couple of hours. We want to find this thing quick before it strikes again."

The feeling in Erik's stomach grew into an icy fist that twisted his insides. A trickle of sweat rolled down the small of his back. He struggled for words, but none came.

"Mr. Simpson? Are you there?"

The ranger's voice brought Erik back. "Sorry. Got distracted. Lindbergh. Two hours. I'll be there."

"Thanks. We really need help on this one."

Erik hung up, hurried to the bathroom and vomited until nothing remained in his stomach. When the sickness subsided, he splashed cold water on his face and returned to the office.

"My God, son, are you all right?" Phineas said when he went back in. "You look like you've seen a ghost."

"Worse."

"You'd better sit down. What was that phone call about?"

Erik took a deep breath and let out a long, shaky sigh. "That was a ranger from Big Pine. There's been an animal attack and they can't figure out what it is. They say it's nothing indigenous. They want our help."

Phineas's eyes grew wide. "Your dream?"

"Look what happened with the tiger."

"Maybe you shouldn't go. I'll take care of it."

Erik shook his head. "I *have* to go. I *have* to know."

"Maybe I'd better come along."

"No sense in the two of us going. One of us has to stay here to cover the offices. I'll be all right." He rested his hand on his father's shoulder. "Don't worry about me. I'm a big boy now."

Phineas smiled weakly. "You'll call?"

Erik nodded, wishing he felt as confident as he sounded.

CHAPTER EIGHT

The sight of pristine mountain lakes and the surrounding scenery normally stirred childlike feelings of joy in Erik, but on this day the mirrored surface of Black Lake stared balefully up at him like the glazed eye of a corpse.

The chopper pilot tapped him on the shoulder and pointed to a small clearing a few hundred yards from the lake. "Wind's unpredictable," he yelled over the drone of the copter blades. "Clearing isn't big enough to set her down. I'll get in as close as I can and lower you in the sling."

A dozen or so rangers and officials in suits milled about the clearing. Erik's stomach spasmed when he recognized the rock above it and the shredded tent from his dream.

The pilot maneuvered the helicopter past the clearing to a small area near the edge of the lake. Hovering above the treetops, he lowered Erik the final fifty feet, putting him down a few yards from shore.

The sound of the copter faded quickly as the pilot flew out of sight, leaving Erik with the smells of pine and the sound of the wind soughing through the trees. He cinched the straps on his day pack, turned and started up the trail toward the clearing.

A short stocky man wearing a ranger's uniform, a Smokey the Bear hat, and mirrored glasses met him part way up the path. A silver nametag above his pocket identified him as LIEUTENANT MITCHELL. A walkie-talkie hanging from his hand periodically ruptured the mountain serenity with blasts of static and conversation.

"Mr. Simpson." Mitchell hung the walkie-talkie on his belt and

34

extended his hand. "Appreciate you coming, especially on such short notice. Anything you want, anything you need, it's yours. We're really stuck on this one."

Erik wiped his sweaty palm on his jeans and took the ranger's hand. "My friends call me Erik."

Mitchell smiled showing perfect teeth. "All right, Erik. My buddies call me Scott. Listen." His voice dropped to a confidential tone. "Like I told you on the phone, we've never seen anything like this. Instead of telling you what I think, it might be better for you to go at this cold. I've instructed my men not to talk to you unless you approach them first."

"Good," Erik said, knowing what he would find and wondering how he could make what he knew from his dream seem like a logical assumption. He knew where to look, but he had to come up with hard evidence.

Mitchell smiled again, then his features hardened. Erik wished he could see what went on behind the sunglasses.

"This way." Mitchell turned and headed back up the path. "Prepare yourself for a lot of blood."

Erik steeled himself, but his stomach felt queasy and his head pounded. He tried to rationalize his discomfort as altitude sickness, but he knew better.

His knees buckled when he saw the remains of the tent at the crest of the trail. A wave of darkness threatened to swallow him.

Mitchell stopped. "You all right?"

"Yeah," Erik said through the haze. "It's the altitude. Coming up from sea level that quick. Haven't had the chance to acclimate."

"I've been up here so long, I forget you lowlanders aren't used to this. Want to rest?"

Erik forced a smile. "No. I'll be okay." He pointed toward the tent. "First I want to get the lay of the area, then I'll start there."

"Mind if I tag along?"

"No problem." Erik started toward the campsite. When he saw the tent, saliva flooded his mouth and he almost vomited. Blood blackened the dirt around the tent. Reddish brown shreds of cloth and stuffing from the sleeping bags lay strewn everywhere. What remained of the nylon had stiffened with crusted blood.

An image of an arm poking out and being ripped from its socket flashed in his mind. He swallowed hard, then circled the remnants of the tent, studying the ground.

"We had to get the remains out of here," Scott said, breaking in on Erik's thoughts. "The smaller animals had already gotten to them."

"Any tracks?"

"Nobody's found any."

Erik nodded, then headed toward the boulder overlooking the clearing. "But you have the equipment if we need it?" he said over his shoulder.

"Absolutely."

He recognized the spot where he and the jaguar had leaped off the rock. When he got to the base of the boulder, he squatted and studied the ground.

"There." He pointed. "Get a man over here with some plaster and make a cast."

"Damn!" Mitchell said under his breath. "Hey, Oppenheimer," he shouted. "Bring the track kit. Our man's struck pay dirt."

A lanky man with curly black hair ran over carrying a small wooden box. He and Erik worked together, meticulously cleaning loose dirt from the track, setting down a ring and pouring plaster. While it dried, Erik and Mitchell climbed up on the boulder and surveyed the clearing.

"It was a cat," Erik said. "He came from up here, smelled the people in the tent, went down and attacked."

"What kind of cat?"

"You saw the print. A big one. You were right. It's not indigenous to this area." He started in the direction the jag had come, retracing the path of the other night. Soon he found more tracks which he marked off for more casts to be taken.

"You're a regular Daniel Boone," Mitchell said. "How did you know he came from this direction?"

Not sure what to say, he blurted, "Instinct."

They went another quarter mile before Erik stopped, his eyes zeroing in on a low hanging branch. "Bingo!" he muttered.

"What?"

He pointed to a tiny clump of black fur caught on the branch. "Our hunter left that. Better get a man up here to bag it so we can bring it back to the lab and confirm what I think."

"You think you know what we're up against?"

"You won't believe me when I tell you."

"Try me."

Erik stood and looked Mitchell in the eye. "We're tracking a jaguar."

"A jag? Up here?" Mitchell let out a low whistle. "How'd he get up here?"

"That's what we'll have to find out. Might have escaped from a wildlife park or from one of those illicit exotic animal collectors. Maybe even an accident with a train or a truck. You better get the word out and see if there've been any reports -- and you better arm your men."

Mitchell took his walkie-talkie from his belt and began giving orders. Two men hurried up. One took casts of the tracks and the other took the hair from the tree branch with tweezers and put it in a bag.

"This is no ordinary jaguar," Erik said as he and Mitchell walked back toward the clearing. Scenes from his dream flashed in his mind, sending a chill down his spine. "Jaguars rarely attack humans."

"But this one does."

"Something must be wrong with it. This is abnormal behavior. If you don't mind, I'd like to take those samples back to San Diego so I can verify my findings, but I'll tell you right now, there's almost no doubt in my mind."

"When can I expect to hear from you?"

"Probably by tonight. I want to talk this over with my father and check out these samples. Shouldn't take long."

They climbed back up on the boulder the jaguar had attacked from and surveyed the clearing.

Mitchell put his hand on Erik's shoulder. "Let me tell you something partner, you're good. Best I've ever seen. Don't have to tell you how much I appreciate your input. How I handle this depends on what you tell me."

Erik flushed, feeling undeserving of Mitchell's praise. He felt guilty for not being honest, but didn't know what to say. Hey, Scott, he thought. I have to be up front with you about this. I was with that jaguar the other night. Those two in the tent were getting it on and their excitement was a little too much for me and the cat. We decided to rip them apart. How was I there? In my sleep. How else? He put his face in his hands. The pounding in his head had escalated to twin jackhammers and his stomach twisted in on itself. He rubbed his eyes, then clutched his stomach.

"You okay?"

"Yeah, I'm okay." He lied. "It's the altitude. Still not used to it."

"You've seen everything you need to see, right?"

Erik nodded.

"Let me see about getting you out of here." Mitchell pulled the walkie-talkie from his belt and called his men together for a meeting in the middle of the clearing. "Stay here and take it easy," he said to Erik. "Once I brief my men we'll get you off the mountain."

"Sure."

Erik went to the edge of the clearing, sat down with his back against a rock, and closed his eyes.

He dozed and lost track of time until the distinct feeling of being stared at brought him out of his stupor. He opened his eyes and locked gazes with a coyote. Its defiant eyes bore into him with an intensity that seemed human. Belligerent. He'd seen many curious animal stares in all the time he spent around them, but nothing like this.

Feeling violated, he returned the scrutiny. The coyote narrowed its eyes, as if showing contempt.

Angered, Erik stood and the coyote bounded off into the brush, leaving him with a feeling that the fuzzy edge of some half-remembered dream had slipped through his fingers like mist.

CHAPTER NINE

With the exception of a few buildings, the San Diego Zoo lay shrouded in darkness. The light from the offices where Phineas and Erik worked blazed in the darkness like a lighthouse beacon. Phineas sat hunched over a microscope studying a slide and making notes on an iPad. Erik sat across the room bent over in a chair, his head in his hands.

"You're right," Phineas said solemnly, looking up from the microscope. "Otorongo, the jaguar. Not characteristic behavior at all." He lowered his voice. "Last time I saw something like this was when you were attacked in the jungle."

Erik forced himself to sit up straight. His stomach still felt queasy, but his headache had diminished to a dull throb. "I don't know what to think anymore. First the dreams, now the phone call. The bloody campsite was eerie enough, but that coyote -- it really spooked me. As absurd as it sounds, it felt like it knew me." He shook off a chill.

"Maybe another session with Dr. Carella will jar something loose?"

"It might, but I'm afraid to tell her everything. She's really something, Dad, but I'm sure she thinks I'm ready for the rubber room. She wouldn't believe me even if I -- what would I tell her? I dreamed of hunting with a jaguar and killed people with it. Oh, and by the way, I had a staring match with a coyote."

"What if I spoke with her?"

"You'll end up in the cell next to mine."

"Hmm." Phineas shook his head. "I don't know what the devil's going on, but I know one thing. You look like hell. Go home to bed.

I'll put a call in to Mitchell in the morning."

"But..."

"We'll talk about it in the morning."

The set expression on his father's face told him the discussion was over. He hadn't seen that look since he was a kid. He couldn't help but smile and relent.

He awoke around ten the following morning. His stomach had settled and his headache had diminished, but his fear lingered. Nicole filled his thoughts like a sun that had the power to burn away the fog.

He grabbed his pants from the chair beside his bed, fished out her number, then grabbed his cell phone from the nightstand and called. After four rings, her voice came on the line.

"You have reached the offices of Carella and Carella. Neither Nicole nor Nicholas can come to the phone at the moment, but if you leave your name and number at the beep, we will get back to you as soon as possible."

Erik started to disconnect, then decided to leave a message.

"Hi, this is Erik Simpson. I called to see about..."

"Erik?" Nicole's voice broke in. "Sorry, the office isn't open today and Dad's out of town. I've been screening our calls. I expected to hear from you sooner. How are you? Where have you been?"

Erik thought of his last twenty four hours and had a strong urge to tell her everything. The throbbing in his head grew. "I had to go up into the mountains and help the rangers identify an animal that attacked some campers."

"Doesn't sound like my idea of fun."

"Something up there bothered me. I know you're not working today, but I was wondering..."

"When can you come in?"

"Um -- well -- how about two?"

"See you then."

After checking in with his father, Erik ate something and left for his appointment. On impulse, he stopped on the way and bought a single rose which he placed carefully in his briefcase.

He stepped into her office at two to find Nicole looking relaxed and casual in jeans and a teal peasant blouse with frilly sleeves. He decided she could do more for a pair of Calvin Klein's than any model. He eyed the vase of flowers on her desk and thought about giving her the rose so he could get it over with, but part of him felt foolish.

She gestured toward a chair. "Please, sit down. Tell me what's going on. I was worried about you after you left the other day."

Between his confusion over his own identity and the strong feelings she brought out in him, Erik struggled to articulate the maelstrom raging inside him. "The past couple days have been rough. I haven't been keeping the greatest hours. Not enough sleep – I mean I'm confused. The feelings inside me. How I feel toward…" He stopped himself.

"You've been through a lot in a short time," she said. "Not keeping regular hours doesn't help. Couple that with having to examine the grisly aftermath of a fatal animal attack, the wild session we had here the other day, and the puzzle of your past -- I'd say you're holding up remarkably well. I don't think I could be as strong as you've been."

Her words washed over him like a soothing balm. Their tone and cool logic drained some of his tension. He kept looking to her for a sign, but each time their gazes met, she looked away.

"Have you had any more dreams?"

He wanted to tell her but couldn't. "No dreams, but seeing what that animal did to those campers shook me up."

"Why don't you take a few days off?"

"My father needs me. We have a lot going on."

She nodded slowly. "Is there anything else you want to tell me?"

Yeah, he thought. You're the most beautiful woman I've ever seen and I want to spend the rest of my life with you. Would you consider going out with a nutcase? "I only wanted to talk," he said. "Dad's a great listener, but I wanted to give him a break. He doesn't show it, but I know he's worried." He remembered the rose and thought of pulling it out.

Her gaze lingered on him for an uncomfortable moment before she turned away. "You're not telling me everything."

Erik sat up straight, jolted.

"But it's okay," she continued, reassuring him. "I don't want you to tell me anything you're not ready to. I want to do this at your pace. You tell me as much as you want, when you feel comfortable about it. No pressure. Okay?"

"Sure. Thanks."

"You should consider taking some time off. When you feel relaxed, give me a call and we'll pick up where we left off. Fair enough?"

"That sounds good. No pressure. And listen. Thanks. Thanks for being here."

She blushed and in that moment he felt an overwhelming tenderness toward her. Give her the damn rose, he thought. Do it!

He stood, grabbed his briefcase, stopped and studied her.

"What is it?" she said softly.

"I'll call you," he said. His voice sounded weak and his legs shook.

She looked up and smiled. "I'll be here. Call me when you're ready to dig some more. In the mean time get some rest."

"Thank you." He turned and left.

Once on the freeway, he opened his briefcase, took the rose and tossed it out the window.

CHAPTER TEN

Erik spent the next few days immersed in his work, trying to distract himself from brooding over Nicole. Mitchell called every day to keep him posted on the hunt for the jaguar, but there had been no sightings and no further attacks. The lack of activity on the jag's part kept Erik on edge, more so because his dreams had stopped.

His sensitivity to what he thought of as the thoughts and feelings of animals had come closer to the surface, making him feel as if he were the guardian of some secret unspoken knowledge. He hoped that by spending most of his time in the company of animals, he would find a clue to his mysterious connection with them. Lately, he felt more at ease in a building full of animals than a room full of people. These feelings brought him to the animal complex at the zoo where he spent most of his afternoons monitoring the tiger's recovery.

One afternoon while making his rounds, he spotted Dr. Hoffelder coming out of the complex. He quickened his pace. "Dr. Hoffelder!" he called. "What are you doing here? Is something wrong with the cat?"

Hoffelder stopped when he saw Erik. "Our patient's fit as a fiddle," he said smiling. "I was in the area and I thought I might drop in to have a look. You've done a good job taking care of him. He's going to be fine." He studied Erik with narrowed eyes. "It's you I'm concerned with, my young friend. You don't look as good as your patient." Hoffelder patted him on the shoulder. "You must not worry so much about that cat. You are worse than an old hausfrau. Besides." He tapped the side of his head with his finger. "If your friend the tiger had any problems, you would know before the rest of us."

Erik saw amusement in the older man's eyes and looked away, embarrassed.

Hoffelder gave Erik's shoulder a firm squeeze. "I have an appointment. You take care of yourself."

"Yeah, sure. Thanks."

"And keep up the good work," Hoffelder called over his shoulder. "Only don't do so much of it."

Erik turned back to the complex and opened the door to the musky scent of animals and their chatter. Sounds and smells that were unpleasant to most came as a unique orchestra to him. He could distinguish each smell and cry, separating them in his mind like a music lover, singling out each instrument, enjoying it both by itself and as a part of the whole.

The prattle increased when he entered, like a group of excited children seeing Santa Claus for the first time. He stifled the urge he always felt to unlock the cages. "Sorry, guys," he said aloud. "I let you out, they lock me up. Besides, it's a crazy world out there. You're safer here."

He ambled down the walkway peering into each cage. Mating chimpanzees in this one, a surly baboon in another. Further down a pair of Koalas clung to each other like teddy bears that had been sewn together. He passed a few birds, a solitary owl, and a pair of lions before coming to the tiger.

The big cat lay at the back of its cage, lounging majestically. When Erik reached the corner of its enclosure, the cat's ears raised and its head swiveled toward him, eyeing Erik with drowsy, feline interest.

"Hey, boy," Erik said softly. "How you feeling today? Doc says you're doing good."

The tiger let out a low growl, hopped to its feet, and sauntered over. When it came to within a few inches of Erik, it sat on its haunches like a trained dog and looked up into Erik's eyes as if to say 'I'm feeling much better, how about you?'

Erik smiled and squatted down until his eyes were level with the cat's. "You'll be getting out of here soon. We have a nice pit fixed up for you. Lots of room to prowl. And you know what?" He lowered his voice conspiratorially. "We got a babe lined up for you."

The tiger's eyes widened and he began to purr.

Without thinking, Erik stuck his hand through the bars and

scratched the cat behind its ear. Only when the tiger squinted did Erik realize the foolishness of his act, yet he felt no fear or desire to withdraw his hand. He sensed the bond between him and the tiger and knew that his actions had been guided by what Phineas called his "special animal ability".

"What is it with us?" Erik said. "You can't talk, but I know what you're thinking and feeling. You're the easy one. Now me, I'm a mess. I've always known it, but it didn't start bothering me until you had your problem. Don't get me wrong, you were hurting, but we cut you open and took your problem out. I wish it were that simple with me." The tiger's eyes rested on him as if giving full attention to his every word.

"You know I've been dreaming about that damned jaguar for years. He's a mean one. The other night I dreamed that I turned into him and we hurt some people -- killed them. A few days later a ranger called asking me to identify it."

The tiger's eyes narrowed again.

Erik stopped scratching its ear and rubbed the top of its head. Its mouth opened in a massive yawn.

"Did I tell you about the lady shrink?" He said, changing the subject. "You're lucky. We pick a mate for you. She's there waiting. Not so easy for me."

The tiger blinked and laid its ears back.

"She thinks I'm a nutcase," he muttered. "But I know better, don't I? I talk things over with a tiger. No offense, boy. You're a better listener that most humans, but you give lousy advice."

The tiger let out a low, satisfied growl, then stretched and lay down against the bars. Erik patted its side.

"Maybe it's time to talk to my Dad. What do you think?" Erik looked down at the tiger. It had fallen asleep.

"I think it's a grand idea."

Erik jumped at the boom of his father's Scottish baritone. "Sorry, son," Phineas said. "Didn't mean to eavesdrop."

Erik looked down the walkway and spotted Phineas.

"I heard your voice," his father said. "And I didn't hear anyone answer. I saw you patting the tiger. I've never in my life seen anyone do that unless the cat was drugged."

Erik smiled sheepishly. "It seemed like the thing to do. How long have you been standing there?"

"I should have made you aware of my presence, but frankly I was quite amazed at what I saw and I didn't want to startle the cat."

Erik stood and brushed himself off. "Well, I've cried on a tiger's shoulder. We both seem to think yours might be better."

Phineas studied the sleeping tiger, then shook his head and put his arm over his son's shoulder. "Tell you what," he said, guiding him out of the complex. "I promise I won't fall asleep."

"Animals have always acted strange around you," Phineas said. Erik sprawled on the couch in the den. Phineas sat back in the leather recliner with his feet kicked up. "Either that or you always acted strange around animals. I've never been able to decide which it is."

"I think it's both." Erik looked up at the artifacts on the wall, feeling comforted by their presence. "It's as if we communicate without words. You know what I mean?"

"Like intuition?"

"That's the closest explanation I can think of."

"And it appears to be growing at a rapid pace. Your recent dreams and your unusual trip to Big Pine prove that."

Erik nodded. "Something's coming to the surface, Dad. Something to do with my past."

"I think seeing Nicole has helped, but she is a distraction. An astonishingly pretty one. That puts you in an awkward spot."

Erik shrugged. "I've been affected by women before, but not like this. Couldn't have come at a worse time. I have enough problems as it is."

Phineas leaned forward and rested his elbows on his knees. "Why don't you tell her how you feel?"

Erik thought of the episode with the rose. "I started to, but I chickened out."

Phineas leaned back in the recliner. "You and I are the only ones who know the whole truth. You're not seeing her because you're schizophrenic or psychotic or anything like that. You're a gifted young man who's beginning to remember his forgotten past. If she knew the whole truth as you and I do, she'd look at you in a completely different light."

Erik nodded. Like always, his father was right.

"I think you should let her know how you feel. The worst she can do is turn you down. If that happens, at least you'll have the satisfaction of knowing the facts. As far as this unfolding of your abilities goes, you have no choice but to ride it out. If you can find it within yourself to separate your problems and deal with the ones you have some control over, it'll remove some of the pressure. This situation has the potential to turn out better than before."

Erik sat up straight. "You're right, Dad. I have to take action on my own."

"That's what I like to hear."

Erik felt a rush of gratitude toward his father that propelled him off the couch and across the room. Leaning over, he hugged Phineas. Before a startled Phineas could speak Erik hurried upstairs to bed.

CHAPTER ELEVEN

Erik went to bed thinking that as much as he feared alienating Nicole, he wanted to let her know his feelings, but he couldn't shake the knowledge of his connection to the jaguar prowling the mountains around Big Pine. How would she react to that? He had been part of a bloody killing. Was he responsible?

He lay awake a long time, not realizing that he had dozed until he started awake, senses altered. Sharpened. A soft breeze slipped over him and the earthy smell of rotting leaves and fresh pine filled his lungs. Mountains. He blinked and his vision came into focus. Though in darkness, his eyesight had an acuity beyond its power in daylight. His ears moved as if raising from his head, zeroing in on the sound of small animals moving in the underbrush. Birds in the trees. Insects.

Looking down, his mind rejected the message his eyes sent to his brain. He closed them, shook his head, and opened them again. Fur. Covering him completely. Paws. A tail. He willed it to move and it flexed as naturally as moving a finger. His tongue found big teeth. Fangs. As strange as it seemed, his sleek body felt as though he belonged in it.

Leaping to his feet, he reveled in the strength and agility with which his body responded. He stepped forward, first slinking, then easing into a swift, loping gait. Muscles flexed beneath skin and fur as his heightened sense of balance carried him with light-footed ease.

Swift and silent, he moved through the woods, stopping only to listen and sniff at the air. Desire gnawed in his gut, driving him onward in search of fresh meat to satiate the blood lust that threatened to overwhelm him. For an instant, he thought his desire odd, but like his body, the instinct felt natural, filling him with terrible hunger.

He heard noises and caught the scent of something in a grove of trees to his right. Pausing, he turned toward the sound and spotted a jack rabbit, poised and immobile at the base of a tree. A rush of saliva filled his mouth. He ran his tongue around cavernous jaws, then hunkered low to the ground, inching toward his victim.

The rabbit moved its head and stopped as if listening before going back to its meal by the tree trunk. Erik moved closer, bracing himself for the final few yards, giving himself to the instinct that burned in the intensity of the hunt.

The rabbit froze, ears lying flat, making no movement except for the rapid rising and falling of its ribs. Erik leaped, surprising himself.

The rabbit bolted, but Erik closed the distance with a few strides. The rabbit cut sharp to the right, then left. Erik closed straight in, pounced and ended the chase.

A high-pitched squeal pierced the night as his jaws closed over the twitching ball of fur. Its ebbing life pulsed between his teeth, feeding his maddening excitement. His fangs clamped down, squeezing, cracking, puncturing. Hot, salty blood pumped into his mouth. He bit and bit again, crushing the body. Holding it between his paws, he ripped it open, baring its quivering pink, gray, shiny organs in the dim light. The tiny heart still quivered.

Shoving his snout into the entrails, he ripped the heart free, savoring its final spurts, then he tore sinew from bone, chewing organs, and swallowing a tangle of fur, fat and muscle, never once questioning his actions.

It wasn't until he lay licking his fur clean, that his rational mind began to function again. A slow dawning realization filled him. There was no question that he had witnessed the slaughter.

He hadn't.

There was no question that he'd been part of it.

He hadn't.

He had been all of it.

The experience had been ecstatic on a savage instinctual level. On a rational level it filled him with loathing. He hadn't been able to control the compulsion.

The split in his nature terrified him. He raised his head to the sky and let out a low mournful cry until the darkness swallowed him and he sat up in bed, sweat streaming from his brow. Wave after wave of confusion rippled through him. In his dream he had been an animal. Hunted. Killed. The most frightening part -- he liked it.

He remembered the frenzy that accompanied the kill and shuddered. With urges that powerful, anything was possible.

CHAPTER TWELVE

Erik spent the morning at UCSD trying to occupy his mind, pecking at the keyboard, stopping from time to time, wondering about his dream. He felt uneasy, as if waiting for disaster. He expected the phone to ring at any moment.

He planned to go to the psychology department to ask Nicole out for lunch. It was the one step he could take toward simplifying his problems.

Maybe I'd better call her now, he thought, glancing at his watch. He pushed his chair away from the desk and reached for the phone. As soon as he touched it, it rang.

His stomach grew cold. He paused, hand hovering over the phone, then it rang again. He snatched it up in mid-ring.

"Hello?"

"Erik. Is that you?"

He heard urgency in Dr. Hoffelder's voice. "What's the matter?"

"The animals. The new shipment."

"They're not due for another week."

"Something has happened. They came early and somehow they've gotten loose. They are running free in the complex."

Erik's chest tightened. "The shipment from Asia? Pit vipers? Cats? Loose?"

"Chimpanzees. Birds. God only knows what else. I heard a ruckus and when I looked in the door I saw a cat roaming the walkway. It's as if the cages have been broken open -- purposely. I've never seen anything like it. I have the building sealed off. I don't think anything's escaped."

"Grab some snake hooks, nooses, and as many tranq guns as you can!"

"I already have some men on it."

"Can you get a copy of the inventory?"

"As soon as I hang up I'll have them send me one. It'll be here by the time you arrive."

"Dad and I will be there inside of half an hour. Don't do anything until we get there."

"You don't have to worry. I have no desire to corral poisonous snakes and tigers."

Erik bolted down the hall and two flights of stairs to where Phineas lectured. Minutes later they sped toward the zoo.

When they arrived, they found the area surrounding the complex roped off. Three zoo security guards patrolled it, keeping people out while watching for stray animals.

A husky, brown-haired guard with a bushy mustache approached them. His nametag said MORALEZ. "Dr. Hoffelder's waiting in your office," he said. "We're pretty sure nothing's escaped, but my men are checking the grounds just the same."

"Good job," Phineas said as he and Erik ducked under the rope. "Don't let anyone in unless we give you the okay."

"Got you covered, Mr. Simpson," Moralez said. "No one's getting by us."

"Thanks."

They found Fritz Hoffelder pacing in the downstairs lab, wringing a handkerchief in his hands. A pile of tranquilizer guns, snake hooks, and animal nooses lay by the door.

Hoffelder stopped pacing and wiped sweat from his forehead when he saw them. "I've never seen anything like this. It looks deliberate."

"Did you get the inventory?" Phineas asked.

"There's no one in the shipper's office. I've been trying to reach an alternate number. Haven't been able to get through."

Erik busied himself loading tranquilizer guns with darts and CO_2 cartridges. "Get security to radio for a cart," Phineas said. "Have them take you to the receiving building. There should be hard copies of the invoices."

Hoffelder hit himself in the head with his palm. "Why didn't I think of that?"

"You were too busy rounding up the gear and notifying security," Erik said. "You did good. Don't be so hard on yourself. You're worse than an old hausfrau."

Hoffelder's head jerked back as if he'd been hit. He frowned at Erik, who winked and grinned. Hoffelder smiled and shook his head, then went out. "I'll return as soon as I can."

"Be careful when you come back," Erik said. "Who knows what we'll find."

"What do you think, Dad?" he said after Hoffelder left.

"It's imperative that we contain the larger brutes first, then make a quick search for anything smaller that looks dangerous. We may not get a chance to reload, but if we can get the biggest animals out of the way, we should be able to round up the rest with hooks and nooses."

Erik finished loading the guns, stuck one in his belt, and held the other. He gave two to Phineas along with a noose and took a snake hook for himself. "Ready?" he said, cocking the pistol.

Phineas nodded.

"Let's do it."

Halfway between the buildings, they heard the pandemonium from the complex. Erik looked back and saw worry lines creasing his father's face. Phineas's eyes hardened as if reading his son's thoughts. He looked toward the door, then put a hand on Erik's shoulder. The firmness of his grip felt reassuring. "Let's get this over with."

Erik peered in the window, cringing at the shrieks and cries that filled the complex. A lifeless gazelle lay in front of the entrance, its ribs and a tangle of viscera exposed at its midsection. Two lions ripped at it, tearing bone and gristle from its side.

"There's a gazelle down in front of the door," Erik said. "Two lions. I'm going to bang on the door and startle them, then I'll whip it open. You should have a clean shot at both."

Phineas positioned himself by the edge of the entrance, raised the pistol and nodded. Erik kicked the door as hard as he could. The two lions leaped backward and Erik yanked the door open. The fear and rage he sensed in the cries of the animals gave him a sick, churning feeling in his gut.

Phineas fired off two darts. The lions jumped and roared, spinning, trying to bite at their flanks where the darts had entered. Erik slammed the door shut and waited until the cats slowed and staggered, finally collapsing.

"Good shot, Dad. Two down."

"Three, counting the gazelle," Phineas muttered. "Let's get in there and get the door shut behind us so nothing gets out."

"I'm with you." Erik stepped in over the remains of the gazelle, followed by his father. The cacophony of animal cries disoriented him as it passed from animal to animal, breaking like a wave. His insides tightened. The musky animal scents smelled sharp and acrid with fear. Erik shook off a rush of dizziness.

"You all right?" Phineas yelled above the din.

"Yeah. I'm fine." Erik crouched, gun in front of him, surveying the building for signs of danger. Beside him, Phineas moved forward, gun ready. Erik followed.

Monkeys chattered and birds fluttered above them. Something screeched. To the right a hyena scavenged the remains of another gazelle. Erik fired a dart into its side. The hyena spun into the air, then ran a few steps before its legs gave.

Together they worked their way through the complex, tranquilizing animals too big and too fast to catch, while rounding up smaller ones using the noose and snake hook.

Toward the end of the building, they split up to trap the remaining animals that took refuge in the corners. Rounding a bend, Erik found himself face to face with a large chimpanzee. When it saw him, it jumped around, hissing and baring its teeth, then it charged, stopping when he raised the gun. Erik and the chimp glared at each other for a long, uncomfortable moment, until the animal backed away and pulled the cage door shut behind it, staring at him the whole time -- with the same defiant humanlike stare he had seen in the coyote.

Once locked in, the look went out of its eyes -- as if another intelligence had left its body.

Erik hustled to the other side of the building where the broken shipping cages were located. He found Phineas on his knees cornering a small cat that had taken refuge behind a crate. Erik came to within a couple of feet of his father and stopped. His breath caught.

A large cobra hovered inches from the back of Phineas's neck, head raised, neck flattened into its telltale hood. "Dad," Erik whispered.

Phineas raised his head and the snake struck the side of his neck. He let out a startled cry and his head hit a crate before he slumped to the ground.

Erik lunged for the cobra, hook extended, but not before it struck

Phineas a second time. He swung the hook full force, knocking the snake aside. It writhed on the floor and raised its head. Erik thought he saw the same defiant gaze in the snake's eyes in the brief instant before it sent a stream of venom into his face, blinding him.

Agonizing pain made him stagger backward screaming. His hands flew to his face and he fell over the prone form of Phineas.

He heard his father's shallow breathing and the snake's slithering, not sure if it came closer, or moved away. He thrashed with his hook as twin bolts of pain drove into his head like white hot stilettos.

"Dad! Dad! You all right?"

No answer.

His heart thumped and his pain rose to a crescendo of exquisite torture. Sobs wracked him and cold sweat ran from his pores like oil.

He heard the snake off to his left. Swung at it. "Dad! Dad! Somebody, help us!" The snake moved again. Erik swung, then heard nothing.

He waited, listening, knowing time to be valuable, wanting to move, yet afraid. He drew himself up on trembling hands and knees, then screamed as the snake's needlelike fangs struck him in the hand.

He swung, felt the hook connect, sensed the weight on the end as he let it fly and heard the snake hit the wall.

He sat up shaking, the pain in his eyes and head maddening him. He had to get out. Get help. He stood, took two steps and stumbled over another crate.

"Erik!" Phineas's voice sounded as if a rag had been stuffed into his mouth."

"Dad."

"Over here."

Erik turned back, trying to force his eyes open. Everything looked as if thick gauze had been wrapped around his head. He dropped to his hands and knees and crawled toward his father's voice. Felt his body and ran his fingers down to the wrist for a pulse.

Weak and irregular.

"Take it easy, Dad. I can't see, but I'm going for help." He ran his hand along his father's torso to his head, raised it and held it in his lap. Phineas gasped. "Feel giddy -- weak. Hard to talk. Swallow."

Erik struggled with the fire in his eyes, forcing himself to see. The blurry image of his father's face swam into view. Phineas's eyelids drooped, giving him a doped, sleepy expression. A string of drool ran down his chin. Tears flooded Erik's burning eyes. He kept them open, forcing himself past the pain. His vision blurred. He laid Phineas's head gently to the floor. "I'm going for help."

Phineas said something, but Erik couldn't make it out. He stood and turned to see the snake blocking his path, head raised, hood open, poised to strike. Erik stumbled backward, grabbing the tranquilizer gun from his pants. "I've had enough of your shit," he said between clenched teeth. "Bite on this!"

The cobra lunged, Erik fired, and a dart flew into the snake's mouth, causing it to coil and writhe on the floor. Erik shot twice more, then dropped the pistol and ran for the door.

With each step he felt darkness closing in until his world reduced to a diminishing circle of light. He staggered forward, falling into blackness.

CHAPTER THIRTEEN

D arkness swallowed him as if he had dropped into the mouth of some huge animal. No feeling. No sound. No sight. No awareness of his surroundings. Only the sensation of falling further into blackness until he became aware of a tiny, pulsing whiteness that beckoned him from off in the distance. He willed himself toward it, and as he drew closer he sensed that the beat of the light matched the rhythm of his heart.

The pulse grew and turned into a beat and the beat into the flapping of wings. An eagle! He recognized it, not knowing from where, only that he knew it intimately and belonged with it.

They flew through the darkness, the eagle both guide and comforter. Erik felt safe and protected in its presence.

Its huge wings beat the air, then spread and sailed on the wind, its piercing brown eyes searching Erik's; both questioning and answering.

Who are you?

"The spirit of your father."

The words came clear, but the eagle's beak never moved. It spoke with its eyes.

Erik remembered Phineas lying on the ground. The snake. Urgency filled him. *You're not... Am I dead?*

"Do not be alarmed, my son. Do not mourn. You are young and strong. You have chosen the sacred animal. It is your guide and protector. Its spirit has chosen you. What has been written into the river of life cannot be changed, not even by death. You must restore the balance."

I don't understand. What are you talking about?

"Face the one who torments you. He has stolen your rightful place among the people, but he knows that it is not his. It belongs to you. He wants to lure you out of your slumber so he can steal your soul and save himself. Take back what is yours."

Steal my soul? What do you mean? Who is after me?

The eagle's eye widened and swirled into geometric patterns. A flurry of images filled Erik's thoughts and his awareness shifted. The black jaguar moved swiftly through the forest in pursuit of a young boy. It leaped and a giant eagle swooped down, catching it in its beak, then rising high into the air. The jaguar squirmed in the eagle's jaws in one moment and in the next shifted its form into a cobra that squirmed and coiled. The eagle let the snake drop from a great height and circled as the cobra disappeared into the blackness.

The fluttering returned. In its center, the eye of the eagle, bright and unchanging, drew Erik up out of the blackness, through a long dark tunnel, closer to the source of light.

He heard voices, barely discernible at first, then stronger.

Dr. Hoffelder's accent. "Flush out his eyes again. The antivenin seems to be taking effect."

The light grew brighter until it hurt. The fluttering continued. "Snake venom opthalmia," another voice said. "But it doesn't look severe. He's responding to the light."

Erik forced his eyes open. The face drew back, taking the tiny flashlight with it. He looked around, and saw the somber face of Dr. Hoffelder, highlighted in the flashing lights of an ambulance.

"Dad! You have to save Dad!" Erik screamed, but his voice sounded far away.

No one moved. No one spoke. He forced his head up and saw two grim-faced paramedics carrying a stretcher with a body on it.

A sheet had been pulled up over the head.

CHAPTER FOURTEEN

Erik sat alone in his father's room staring at the walls, listening to the silence that had become his companion. His whole being felt empty, his numbed thoughts and emotions suspended like bubbles in oil.

Alone.

No family. No connection to his past. No one but himself and an empty house. Nothing to fill the nothingness.

He had donated most of his father's clothes to charity, but the room still smelled of Phineas. The things Erik couldn't bear to give away lay before him on the bed. Old books, a box of pictures, a pipe that Phineas smoked on rare occasions, his favorite hat, a walking stick that had been with him on all his expeditions; and a box of old leather bound journals.

Erik moved in a daze, packing most of what lay on the bed into a box that he stored in the back of the closet until the pictures and journals remained.

He picked up the box of pictures, started toward the closet, then on impulse, set it back on the bed. The first photos he came across were a young Phineas and his bride, the mother Erik had known for a few fleeting weeks before she died. More pictures of a young Phineas graduating college, an older Phineas lecturing, group pictures of expeditions in different parts of the world, then a handful of pictures that made Erik's throat constrict. He recognized the wild-eyed boy with the tangled hair beside Phineas wearing nothing but face paint, a loincloth and an amulet. Reaching into his shirt, he pulled out the claw, tooth and amber charm, then looked back at the picture. His face had been painted like the ceremonial masks hanging in the den. In front of the group lay the body of a huge black jaguar.

He looked through more pictures of Phineas teaching him how to eat with a knife and fork. His first haircut. Lord, how he'd hated that. He remembered his first pair of pants, how uncomfortable they felt, and the conflicting emotions they stirred in him. The trappings of civilization felt restricting, yet at the same time familiar, as if belonging to a forgotten time in another world. He learned language with an ease that indicated he was not learning it for the first time, but rediscovering it.

"Phin-ee-aas. Come on say it, boy." The bearded man jabbed himself in the chest. "Phin-ee-aas. I know you can say it."

"Phinn-eee-aas," Erik repeated. The word sounded strange, but felt natural the way it floated off his tongue. "Phinneeaas," he said again and giggled. This game was fun. "Phineas." He pointed at the older man.

Phineas reared his head, let out a hearty laugh, and slapped his knee. "Phineas. You've got it, son." He leaned forward, crossing his arms. "You need a name. With that head of hair and those wild blue eyes, you remind me of a Swedish fellow I used to know. Erik." He poked the boy gently in the chest with his finger. "Erik. That's what I'll call you. E-rik." He poked again, emphasizing the two syllables. "E-rik." He jabbed himself in the chest. "Phineas."

Erik imitated his movements, pointing to himself, saying, "Erik." Then pointing to his father.

"Phineas," Erik whispered. A tear splashed onto the picture. He tried to stifle his sorrow, then gave up.

When his grief subsided, he sorted through the rest of the photos, reliving each moment frozen on film in hopes of stirring more than grief, but each picture only sent him deeper into depression.

When he threw the pictures back into the box, one flew over the top. He picked it up and did a double take. Something about it looked strange. Another group picture. Flipping it over he read his father's faded printing on the back.

"Erik's birthday."

He turned the photo over again and laid it on the bed, puzzling over it. Phineas stood in the center, beaming, one arm draped over the boy's shoulder. Erik sported a new haircut and clothes that were too big.

There were other men. Professor types like Phineas and a few Indians. What was it? He studied each man in detail, his features, his expression. They all appeared normal, then -- one of the Indians standing off to the side. A young boy – a little older than Erik.

His eyes burned into the camera. A defiant stare. Full of contempt, the same as...

An icy chill slithered down his spine. He threw the picture back into the box face down.

After a sleepless night, he drove to Nicole's Del Mar office and sat outside the door. She found him dozing when she came in at ten.

"What are you doing here?"

His eyes popped open and darted back and forth, frantically searching for the threat.

"You all right?"

"Yeah, I'm okay," he mumbled. "Couldn't sleep. Didn't know what to do."

"I've been trying to reach you for days. You had me worried." She unlocked the door and beckoned. "Come in. Let me fix you some coffee."

He slumped into a chair and stared at the floor while Nicole started the coffee maker.

"I came to see you in the hospital," she said, breaking the silence, "but they wouldn't let me in because I wasn't family. From what the doctors told me, you're very lucky. You came close to dying. It's a miracle your eyesight wasn't permanently damaged."

"They didn't let me go to the funeral."

"Doctors here in the States don't have much experience with cobra bites. From what they told me, lung paralysis can occur up to ten days after the injury. They didn't want to take the risk. It was a nice ceremony. Short and to the point, the way he would have wanted it."

Erik looked up. "You went?"

Nicole handed him a cup of coffee. "I know you have no family, but you couldn't tell by the turnout. A lot of people are going to miss him."

"He wants me to scatter his ashes over the mountains."

"There, you see? You missed the funeral, but you'll have the last moments alone with him."

"So much I wanted to say," Erik whispered. "So much I wanted to tell him. How much I loved him. If only..."

"If only what?"

"It's my fault he's dead."

"Why do you say that?"

Hot tears blurred his vision. "I'm a zoologist. I'm supposed to be the wonder boy who knows all about animals. I saw the snake and opened my big mouth. It bit him. I should've been more careful." A sob rose in his throat, but he fought it back.

"You're not being fair to yourself. What happened isn't your fault. You had no way of knowing..."

"I'm supposed to know!" Erik said. "That's what I do."

"You can't blame yourself."

"You don't know what you're talking about. It's easy for you to sit behind your desk, so cool, so professional, never letting me know how *you* feel. And me, like an idiot, I come and spill my guts."

She looked at him wide-eyed, her face pale. "You're not being fair to yourself or to me," she said turning away.

"I'm sorry. I'm upset. I feel so many things about my father and about you."

"Me?"

He heard a tremor in her voice, but his pain made him feel embarrassed and exposed.

"I can't take this anymore." He pushed his chair back. "I have to get out of here."

Nicole stood and reached across the desk. "Don't go. You're not alone."

Erik yanked his hand back, and stormed out of the office.

CHAPTER FIFTEEN

E rik sat in the kitchen of the townhouse staring at a fifth of Seagram's Seven. He never liked liquor, its taste, or the way it made him feel, but he couldn't stand being alone for another moment.

He poured a shot and downed it, gagging at first, then letting its fire kindle in his belly. The spreading warmth felt good. He poured another and tipped it up. The second one went down easier. He gulped a third, welcoming the numbing warmth that seeped into his brain. After three shots, his emptiness wasn't so unbearable, so he drank a fourth.

Seven shots later he took the phone off the hook, grabbed the urn holding his father's ashes and slumped into the easy chair in the corner of the den.

"Why'd you have to go?" he muttered, slurring his words. "I'm not ready to be alone. You think I'm some kind of wunderkind, but I'm not. I'm a loser. It's my fault you're gone."

Tears welled in his eyes. He was tired of crying. He felt numb, deadened, and empty, like he had no grief left to give, yet tears spilled, out of control. He hugged the urn and rocked back and forth letting the sobs ripple through him.

When they subsided, he wiped his face with the back of his hand. "I'm not going to let you down," he said to the urn. "Tomorrow I'm taking you up to the mountains and giving you back to God."

His stomach churned and bile rose in the back of his throat. He forced himself up and staggered to the bathroom, making it just in time.

After throwing up, he shuffled into Phineas's room clutching the urn. Collapsing on the bed next to the box of journals, he held the urn close and draped his other arm around the journals.

He woke up dehydrated, the light from the window stabbing into his brain. His head throbbed, his stomach felt queasy, and his mouth gummy. He knew why he hated alcohol. The silence greeting his awakening weighed on him. He looked from the urn to the box of journals, then to the empty room.

The realization of his loss returned full force, rocking him as though he'd been punched in the stomach. He forced himself to sit up, fighting back dizziness.

"Enough!" he said through gritted teeth. "Can't stand being here. Can't keep going like this." He addressed the urn again. "Gotta let you go, Dad. It's the only way either of us are going to get any rest."

He felt better after showering, but his head still pounded and his stomach felt jumpy. He took three aspirin, made coffee and forced himself to eat.

Halfway through his meal he vomited again.

An hour later he managed to keep two pieces of toast down and his headache had diminished to a dull throb that flared only when he exerted himself.

He moved through the house dragging his backpacking gear out of the closets and loading his pack with food and clothes. When it was almost full, he went back to his father's room to get the urn lying on the bed next to the journals.

"Shit," he said under his breath. "I have to deal with those. Don't want to do it when I get back."

He sat on the edge of the bed and went through the box, skimming each volume. Most of were diaries of Phineas's expeditions. At the bottom of the pile, the title of one of them jumped out at him.

SOUTH AMERICA/ERIK PHENOMENON

He read the first few pages; Phineas's account of the jaguar chase. It read the same way Phineas told it.

Never knew he wrote it down, Erik thought. He skimmed more pages of his father's observations about his time in college, then flipped to the end and found the most recent entry describing the day Erik had been patting and talking to the tiger.

He stored the rest of the books in the closet, grabbed the urn and diary, and stuffed them into his pack. After loading the rest of his things into the car, he locked the house and glanced back for a wistful moment, then took a deep breath and turned away. "I'm out of here."

He drove north from San Diego, not sure where he was going, only that he wanted to escape into the mountains. Anywhere in the High Sierras -- except Big Pine. Dad wants his ashes scattered in the mountains, he thought. And he deserves the best and the highest.

He reached Lone Pine some time after midnight and parked in front of the ranger station. An hour after it opened, he stood at the trail head at Whitney Portal adjusting the straps on his pack.

A light breeze whispered in the pine boughs above, carrying with it the invigorating freshness of the mountains he and Phineas loved so much. The morning felt cool when he set out, but the sun rose quickly.

Moving steadily up the trail, he passed a few people, but as he gained elevation, contact became less frequent. He stopped for lunch at Mirror Lake. His breathing came harder and the beginnings of a headache burrowed into his skull, only this time he knew the altitude had thinned the oxygen in his blood. Even the trees were stunted.

Pressing on, he made Trail Camp by nightfall. The rocky terrain looked like a surrealistic moonscape in the fading glow of sunset. Nothing lived up here except scavenging marmots, chipmunks, moss, and a few stubborn weeds.

He made a quick dinner, hung his food from a high rock and climbed into his sleeping bag, hands clutching his head. In spite of his exhaustion he didn't sleep much. The pain had doubled since lunch.

He arose in darkness and started his final ascent up the treeless mountainside with a day pack carrying food, water, and the urn. The pile driver in his head continued unabated. His stomach churned. He stopped to catch his breath when dizziness made him totter and see spots and he vomited twice. When nothing remained in his stomach, he pushed harder, promising himself that he would make the summit before the sun came up.

When he reached the barren peak of Mount Whitney he stood alone, the world spread out beneath him. The wind blew strong, the air cold and bracing. A red-rimmed horizon glowed in the east, casting its feeble light into the blue of the sky. No moon. Behind him to the west lay the darkened shroud of passing night.

He fumbled through his pack with trembling hands, pulled out the urn, and took off its cover. The wind gusted as if in concert with his actions. Holding the urn above his head, he let the wind buffet him, blowing tears across his cheeks.

A tiny spark of gold glimmered on the eastern horizon. Erik's chest tightened. He sobbed and raised the urn still higher. His tears flowed heavier.

"God bless you, Dad!" he cried, spinning in a circle, sending his father's ashes flying into the wind. Once empty, he dropped to the ground and closed his eyes.

He awoke on his back, the morning sun hot on his face, the empty urn beside him, the feeling of being watched pressing on him.

Slowly, he raised his head to see a magnificent eagle perched on a rock a few feet away, studying him. Its eyes did not hold the defiant, contemptuous stare he had come to dread. This looked like an understanding gaze. The one he had seen in his delirium after the cobra bite.

"Dad!" he gasped and the eagle took wing. Its huge form sailed into the air, circling the peak in ever increasing spirals until it found a spot directly above him where it floated effortlessly on the currents, majestic wings outstretched.

The sight thrilled Erik. Hope swelled in his chest and in that moment his feeling of aloneness vanished, replaced by a gentle calm. He gathered his things and started down the mountain, periodically checking the skies. The eagle remained high in the air directly above as though watching over him.

He stumbled into Trail Camp feeling lightheaded and hungry. His headache had gone. He looked up once more at the soaring eagle, then too exhausted to eat, he climbed into his tent and fell asleep, not waking again until the predawn hours of the following morning.

He felt worn and fragile, his legs weak, but he felt at peace. His loneliness remained, only now it seemed bearable. Something he could learn to live with. He dressed slowly, then pushed back the flap of his tent.

The chill air of a stark Sierra morning met him. He stood and studied the huddled masses of boulders, then gazed up at the stars strewn across the darkened sky and wondered about Phineas. A shooting star sailed overhead as if answering his thought.

Later that day he hiked down to a lower altitude. He saw no sign of the eagle. Finding a pleasant spot within walking distance from a stream, he set up camp, made dinner and ate ravenously.

After hanging his food for the night, Erik broke out his lantern and found a comfortable spot beneath a tree to settle down with his father's journal. He skimmed the beginning again, then read Phineas's diary of what happened after the incident with the jaguar. After several paragraphs of speculation as to Erik's origin, notes followed, observing his behavior.

8/9

I have decided to call the boy Erik because his blond hair and blue eyes make me think he is Scandinavian. I believe he is around twelve. The amulet he wears is puzzling. Amber with two claws and two fangs protruding from four sides. From a jaguar.

In spite of his wildness and uncivilized behavior he learns amazingly fast; as if this is not his first time being taught. More like he's remembering. He learns seven or eight words a day. I suspect this number will increase dramatically.

8/10

I cannot believe how quickly he learns.

8/11

Erik seems to have a strange rapport with animals.

Today I saw him pick up a wild monkey. The monkey showed no fear and it trusted him completely. Later in the day a bird flew overhead. Erik held out his hand and it came to him. He doesn't seem to think this strange and acts quite casual about it.

8/14

Today my suspicions were confirmed in a most unsettling manner! I went to wake him this morning and found him asleep with a baby howler monkey, a jaguar cub and several smaller animals cuddled around him like stuffed animals. I woke him by gently calling his name. The animals dispersed when he opened his eyes.

8/15

I have reason to believe that the same eagle has been following us through the jungle since the day Erik came screaming out of the woods. If I didn't know better, I'd say it was watching him.

Erik dropped the journal in his lap and felt the amulet beneath his shirt. The events of the last few months flashed through his mind. The jaguar dreams, his experience with the tiger, the sessions with Nicole, his animal imitations, his dreams of hunting, the coyote that stared at him, the glares of the chimpanzee and cobra that nightmarish day in the compound -- and the amulet. He pulled it out from his shirt and studied it.

It all pointed to something. Something about him. He still couldn't grasp its significance, but he felt as if the answers hung just out of reach.

CHAPTER SIXTEEN

Not ready to face the emptiness awaiting him at the house, Erik drove through the night from Lone Pine, arriving at the zoo a couple of hours before daylight. After checking in with security, he stood between the animal complex and the office, trying to decide where to go first.

An image of the cobra striking Phineas flashed in his mind, making his hands shake. He remembered the way it studied him -- and the chimp. His mouth went dry. Same look. He wasn't ready. Maybe he never would be.

He thrust his hands into his pockets and strode away. Instead of going back to his car, he found himself walking past the Reptile House, down toward Tiger River. The morning sun glowed crimson on the horizon and the musky animal smells drifted to him on the moist morning air, soothing him.

The Bengal tiger he had "communicated" with slept in a large pit at the bottom of the hill. Careful not to disturb it, he approached quietly, remembering his connection with it. He took a deep breath and let it out slowly. This is it, he thought. Trust. Grabbing the lip of the wall, he hefted himself over it and dropped into the pit, landing nimbly on his feet.

The tiger leaped up, spotted him and growled, then crouched low, laid its ears back and crept toward him.

Fully aware of the irreversibility of his act, Erik steeled himself. The tiger broke into a trot, heading straight for him. Erik concentrated on it and a strange calmness descended over him. Narrowing his gaze, he met the glare of the cat. It stopped as if it had been hit, straightened, and sidled up to him, rumbling with a contented purr. Erik held his arms out and the tiger stood on its hind legs and draped its paws over his shoulders.

Grunting under its weight, Erik hugged it and felt a surge of empathy toward the beast. "Hey, buddy." He stroked the tiger's neck. "I missed you."

The cat drew its head back, studied Erik a moment, then licked him.

"Ho, partner, you're too big for me." He pushed the tiger off and wiped his face with his sleeve. The big cat passed back and forth in front of him, rubbing its flank against his legs.

Erik ruffled the fur on its head, then trotted around the cage, the tiger following like a pet. He found a small branch and waved it in front of its head. The tiger rolled onto its back and batted at the stick like a kitten, claws sheathed. When he tired of the game, Erik sat in the corner of the pit with his back against the wall. The cat came and lay beside him, putting its head in his lap. He patted it, then dozed, slumping forward, falling asleep on top of it.

He heard voices from far away, recognizing one as Dr. Hoffelder's.

"You did the right thing calling me."

"I didn't know what else to do. The tiger must have killed him, but there's no blood."

"I wouldn't be so sure," Hoffelder said. "Erik has a way with animals."

"I don't think so," the second man said. "I'll tranq the tiger, then we'll find out."

Erik opened his eyes and looked up to see Hoffelder, Moralez the security guard, and a group of zoo employees huddled by the edge of the pit. Moralez had a tranquilizer rifle to his shoulder, ready to fire. Erik held up both hands and waved. Shocked expressions spread across the faces in the group.

Moralez lowered the gun, mouth open in amazement. Hoffelder shook his head.

Erik leaned forward and whispered in the tiger's ear. "I know you don't understand my words, but I think you understand my thoughts. Lie here like you're sleeping. Let me do the talking."

The tiger opened one eye and purred, then closed it. Erik couldn't be sure the cat understood, but he had a feeling it did. Lifting its massive head from his lap, he slid out from beneath it and gently laid it back on the ground.

"Thanks, buddy," he whispered, stroking its side.

He went to the edge of the pit to deal with his unwanted audience. "Sorry, he's already been sedated. I came to check on him and found a problem. I wanted to take a closer look, so I tranqued him. It wasn't very smart of me to fall asleep, but I couldn't help it. I was exhausted."

One of the guards shook his head and walked away. Erik studied the rest of the group, watching their confusion register as each accepted his lie. No one gave any sign of doubt, except Hoffelder, who scrutinized Erik, his eyes full of questions. Erik smiled sheepishly, then turned and went to the rear of the pit to let himself out.

"Good thing one of my men saw you before we opened the gates," Moralez said as Erik came around to the front. "Can you imagine what would have happened if some school kid had seen you sleeping down there?"

"Sorry," Erik said. "That was really stupid. I was worried about the cat."

Moralez shrugged. "No harm done. You guys better get to work," he said addressing the crowd. "Zoo opens in ten minutes." The crowd drifted away murmuring among themselves, leaving Erik, Moralez, and Hoffelder behind.

Moralez gripped Erik firmly on the shoulder and looked into his eyes. "You feeling all right?"

"I'm okay, thanks. Just tired. A little behind on my sleep."

"Listen, I'm sorry about your Dad. We did what we could."

"I know," Erik said. "I appreciate everything you did." He looked at Hoffelder, then back to Moralez. "If it wasn't for you guys I wouldn't have made it."

"I worked with him for years," Moralez said. "We're all gonna miss him. If there's anything you need, anything I can do, even if it's just talking or getting plastered together, you let me know." He handed Erik one of his business cards.

Erik took the card and slipped it into his pocket. "Thanks, Tony, I appreciate that."

"No problem. I have to get back to work. You guys need a ride?"

Erik looked at Hoffelder, who studied him with his arms crossed, then back to Tony. "That's all right. We'll walk."

Moralez nodded, climbed into his cart, and pulled away.

Erik turned to Hoffelder, who rocked back and forth on his heels, arms still crossed.

"I don't know what it is about you, Erik," he said quietly, "but I know that tiger is not sick and I am pretty sure it is not sedated. I've been watching you since you were a boy. I know you have this special gift." Hoffelder pointed to his head. "Your father knew, but never talked about it. I've had my suspicions, but never asked. Your father is gone now. Whether you want to talk to me or not is your business, but I think it might be a good idea. All I can give you is my word that I will tell no one."

Erik eyed the older man. In all the years they worked together, Hoffelder had witnessed a lot, but he always respected Erik's privacy. There had been times when he could have pushed for an explanation, but never had.

"You're right," Erik said. "I can trust you. That hasn't been a worry. It's just that -- well it's all so strange."

Hoffelder chuckled. "No offense, Erik, but there is a lot about you that is strange."

Erik smiled and gestured. "Feel like walking? This is going to take awhile."

It took a few hours, but he told everything while Hoffelder listened, adding his own thoughts and observations which gave his growing self-knowledge another dimension. By the time he finished, they had made a complete circuit of the zoo, ending in front of Erik's office beside the compound. Erik stopped and stared at the two buildings. His legs felt weak.

"I don't think I'm ready to go in yet," he said.

Hoffelder nodded. "Don't worry. I've been taking care of things since the accident. I can handle them for awhile longer." He pointed toward the compound. "If what you say is true, then what happened in there has something to do with your abilities. Let me know if there's anything I can do to help."

"You've done enough already. I don't know how to thank you."

"By coming back to work with me when you're ready." His eyes brightened. "I am not embarrassed to say that I would be most honored to work with you. Your link with animals makes you very special." He clapped his hands together like a child. "A lot of good can be done with it."

"Thanks, doc. I have a few things to figure out first. Once I get a handle on them, you have yourself a partner."

"Take your time. If you need to talk, I'm here. And let me give you one last bit of advice if I may."

"What's that?"

"Go home and get some rest, then talk to that woman you've been working with. You owe her that."

They shook hands before Hoffelder disappeared into the compound.

Erik felt as if some of his burden had lifted and with the removal of the weight came an awareness of how tired and hungry he was. Looking down at himself, he saw that his clothes were rumpled and dirty. He sniffed at his armpit and wrinkled his nose. He needed a shower too. Best go home, clean up, and get some sack time.

CHAPTER SEVENTEEN

After eating and showering, Erik slept until the following afternoon. When he awoke, the silence that greeted him felt strange. He half expected Phineas to come through the door, but the quiet remained unbroken.

A surge of excitement filled him as the previous day's experience flooded his mind. He had consciously reached out with his thoughts and touched the tiger's mind with his own. Could he do it with any animal?

He thought of the hostile animals that seemed to touch his mind, as if they contained an intelligence beyond normal. Was it a two way street? He decided to go to the zoo that night to find out.

Later that night he pulled in to the zoo parking lot. After checking in with security, he went to his office, pausing outside before forcing himself to go in. It looked the same as it had the day Phineas died.

He dropped into his chair and closed his eyes, half expecting to open them and see his father moving about the office, shuffling through his notes, talking to himself.

He took a quick glimpse into his father's office, then made his way to the compound, not sure if he was ready to face the aftermath of his father's death.

The cool night air made him realize he was sweating. His hands shook when he touched the cold metal of the door. Putting his face to the window, he peered into the blackness, seeing nothing.

He took a deep breath, pulled the door open and stepped into the darkness. The familiar animal smells heightened his senses. He hit the light switch by the door, illuminating the compound and the building came alive with the sounds of screeching and chattering that seemed to scold him for disturbing their sleep. Different animals inhabited the cages than the ones that had been there the day Phineas was bitten.

A pair of tiny Rhesus monkeys huddled together in a corner of the first cell watching him in wary-eyed silence. Erik leaned against the bars of the cage and gazed back, sending forth warm thoughts. The two monkeys scuttled toward him. One climbed the bars until it came level with his head, reached out a tiny paw and touched him on the face, its eyes imploring. Erik shook off a warm shiver. The monkey's look reminded him of an adoring mother.

The second monkey tugged on the leg of his pants. When Erik looked down, it gave him a monkey-smile, then capered around the cage chattering happily. When it made a complete circuit it climbed up next to his face and stroked his hair.

"How you guys doing?" he asked. "They treating you good?" He stuck his hand through the bars and took turns patting them.

"You two go back to sleep," he said, giving them a final pat. "I'll be around later."

The monkeys chattered quietly, then jumped down and went back to their corner holding hands.

Two cages down he came across a huge Sun Bear slumbering near the front of its enclosure. This ought to be a good test, he thought, clapping his hands. The bear rolled to its feet, raised its snout and bellowed. Huge dark eyes searched for the source of the noise until its gaze found Erik, who repeated what he had done with the monkeys. The bear let out a low moan and lumbered over to the front of the cage.

Erik felt a quiver of excitement when he patted the bear's thick hide. It stuck its snout through the bars and nuzzled his face, slobbering on his cheek. Its hot breath smelled like fishy garbage. "Whoa, partner. Ain't you ever heard of Listerine? Whew." Erik waved his hand in front of his face and laughed. "Sorry to wake you, but I had to know. I'll leave you alone now so you can go to sleep." The bear drew back, giving him a reproachful look.

Erik went through the compound repeating the ritual with a rhino, a condor, two lynxes and a baboon. Some animals seemed shyer than others, but all came to him unafraid, their trust complete.

Elated, he went outside and walked the zoo grounds, stopping at the cages where he saw activity. To his delight, he found he could "touch" animal minds even in the darkness without eye contact.

He left the zoo some time after midnight, went home and waited for morning, unable to sleep. In the den he drank hot chocolate, pondering his discovery.

Stretching out in his father's recliner, Erik closed his eyes, trying to figure out how his discovery fit in with everything that happened. He knew there was a connection, but he couldn't make it.

This time he hadn't come across any hostile animals like the snake or chimp. What would happen if he ran across one now that he knew what he could do? The chimp had backed down, but the cobra didn't. Both seemed to defy him.

He drifted off into a light, dreamless sleep, his last conscious thought was of a cobra writhing in the beak of an eagle.

CHAPTER EIGHTEEN

Erik awoke to the heat of the morning sun streaming through the window. A sheen of sweat covered his body and his throat felt scratchy. He rubbed his eyes and looked at the time on his cell phone. Ten-thirty. He tapped his Contacts icon and called Dr. Hoffelder.

"Erik," Hoffelder said when he picked up. "Is everything all right?"

"There's something I need to show you. Are you at the zoo?"

"I'm here working."

"I'll be right over."

He found Dr. Hoffelder working on a sedated lemur in the treatment room beside the complex.

"Almost finished," Hoffelder said. "Our little friend here had an infection, but it will be fine now." He patted the lemur, looked up and smiled.

"I've been thinking," Erik said. "I need my father's notes and stuff, but I don't need his work area. I'm going to clean out his desk and office this weekend so we can have a place to work together."

Hoffelder smiled broadly and pulled off his gloves. "I see good things for us in the future, my friend. Now I know you didn't make this appointment just to give me this good news. You have something to show me?"

Erik smiled. "Do I ever."

Fritz looked at his watch. "Can you wait a few more minutes? I'm waiting for someone."

"Who?"

"Me," Nicole said, sticking her head through the door.

Erik froze, mouth open. "What the?"

She reached out and hugged him. Her warmth and the smell of her hair intoxicated him. "Erik," she said softly, "I know how you feel about me. Your father told me before he died." She looked up at him. "I have the same feelings, but I shouldn't get involved. I can't let it get in the way of helping you." She glanced at Dr. Hoffelder. "It's not only unprofessional, but dangerous, although Dr. Hoffelder seems to think differently."

Fritz shrugged and his face reddened. "She called looking for you. I remembered what you told me about her. She and I discussed your abilities and I told her about the tiger. She thought I was joking until she talked to Sgt. Moralez."

"He still thinks you drugged the cat," Nicole added.

Fritz nodded. "When I knew you were coming, I thought, well maybe..."

"I owe you both an apology. I've been too wrapped up in self-pity to see that you guys were there." He looked from Fritz to Nicole. "I'm really sorry."

Fritz made a dismissive gesture. "Don't worry about it. You lost your father. That's not easy for anyone to deal with. Especially someone like you. He was all you had, but it is time for you to move on with your life."

"Now what's this big secret of yours?" Nicole said, stepping back and crossing her arms.

"I want each of you to pick an animal."

"Any animal?" she asked.

"Doesn't matter if it's dangerous or..." An image of the cobra striking Phineas flashed in his mind. "Except a snake."

Hoffelder picked up the limp body of the lemur. "I'll have one by the time I get back. I have to put this little fellow back in his cage before the sedation wears off."

Inside the compound, Fritz set the lemur gently on the floor of a cage and closed the door behind him. "That takes care of business," he said. "Now let us see what this is all about."

"What animal did you pick?" Erik said, grinning.

Fritz nodded toward Nicole. "Ladies first."

"I don't know." She put a finger to her lips and studied the cages.

"How about him?" She pointed to the Sun Bear sitting on its haunches in the corner of its enclosure.

Erik rolled his eyes. "You *would* pick him. Okay. Stay right here and promise you won't move, no matter what happens. Do I have your word?"

Fritz and Nicole nodded in unison.

"Hey, doc, can I borrow your keys?"

Hoffelder frowned and tossed a key ring to him. Erik approached the bear, thinking friendly thoughts until he "felt" the bear giving back amiable thoughts of its own. Satisfied, he unlocked the door and let himself into the cage to the sound of Nicole's gasp and Fritz's surprised grunt. He walked straight to the bear, put his arm around its neck and hugged it. The bear draped a paw over his shoulder and stared back, its eyes searching.

"We're buddies," Erik said, patting the bear's back. "We understand each other's thoughts. I'm sure he doesn't know words or anything. It's more primitive. Like we feel each other's emotions."

"Amazing," Fritz said. He and Nicole edged closer. "That explains you and the Bengal."

"Don't get too close. This is still new for him. You might spook him."

"How long have you known this?" Nicole asked.

"I discovered it last night." The bear started licking the side of Erik's face. "Uuuh. He's got a serious case of halitosis."

Nicole giggled and the bear raised its snout in the air and let out a low moan.

Erik stroked the back of its head. "I think he likes you."

"And you can do this with any animal?" Fritz asked, wide-eyed.

"Every one I've tried so far."

"Amazing."

Erik disengaged himself and started toward the cage door. The bear followed. Nicole held her hand over her mouth and pointed. Erik turned and the bear stopped. "Sorry, buddy, as much as I'd like to free you, I can't."

The bear moaned again.

"I know, but believe me, it's safer in here." He let himself out, went to two other cages and repeated the routine with the Rhesus monkeys and the rhino, noticing that the animals were more apprehensive with strangers around, but they all trusted him.

"This is incredible!" Nicole said when the three of them went back to the office. "This could be a major breakthrough with your amnesia. And it fits in with those animal imitations you did. Are you ready to try another hypnosis session?"

CHAPTER NINETEEN

E rik picked up a rose on the way to Nicole's office the following morning. After carefully placing it in his briefcase, he hustled up to her office.

"Come in," she said, gracing him with a tender smile. She looked stunning in a pink chiffon blouse and lavender blazer.

Erik laid his briefcase on her desk, popped the snaps and produced the rose.

"Thank you." She took it, closed her eyes and sniffed the bud.

Erik watched her put it in a vase. "Will you have dinner with me tonight?"

"Yes," she said, smiling with her eyes. "We'll talk about our situation then." Her expression grew serious. "Now I want to talk about you." She gathered up her note pad and recorder and gestured toward the recliner.

Moments later, the sound of the ocean filled the room. Erik struggled to concentrate on the penlight without looking at her. In spite of his difficulty, he went under easier than he had the first time...

...waking to Nicole's soft features. Seeing her made him smile and wonder what it would be like to see her like this every morning.

He had the dreamlike feeling of something he should have remembered, but nothing came to mind. He searched her face for a hint of anything new, but saw nothing. Instead, she looked lost in thought. He wanted to question her, but held back.

A moment later, her eyes came into focus. She leaned forward and pointed to the cassette. "I know this sounds strange, but you went through your childhood again, then you went through the animal sounds. We hit that same -- the only way I can describe it is a wall that's blocking your past, but this time I think we touched something on the other side."

"What was it?"

"You said a few words that sounded familiar. I think they were Spanish, but they didn't make any sense. I'm hoping they might jog your memory when you hear them."

"I felt like I was trying to remember something when you brought me out of the trance."

She tapped buttons on the recorder until Erik heard himself making animal sounds and Nicole's soft voice coaxing him to reach back further, then the cries stopped, followed by silence, then disjointed words and phrases in a strange dialect. Nicole tried coaxing him more, but he didn't respond.

"That's it," she said jabbing a button.

The words echoed in Erik's mind, sending a surge of confusion and excitement through him. "Play it again!"

She played back the sounds. Erik made her replay them three more times, then leaned back and closed his eyes. The sights, sounds, and smells of the jungle rushed into his mind. And the words.

"Vision Vine," he said aloud. "The Vine of the Soul. The Holy Flower of the North Star. The Sacred Cactus of the Four Winds. The Flying Death. Time to die as a boy. Become a man. The battle of the two sides of spirit. Behold the wonder of the sacred vision. You will meet your spirit animal and he will show you the path. He who has the vision is the brother of the sacred animal. The one who must lead." He opened his eyes.

"What does it mean?"

He rubbed his eyes with balled fists. "I have to find out what the Vision Vine is. What it means."

"Is there someone in the biology department who would know?"

"Dr. Gilbert," he blurted. "Head of the botany department. He was part of the expedition when my father found me." He got up from the recliner, leaned over, and kissed Nicole on the cheek. "Thanks I have to go."

"What about tonight?"

"I'll pick you up at eight."

Erik recognized the heavy-set, balding man from the tufts of wispy hair covering the side of his head. Gilbert's prominent pot belly, bifocals, white hair and beard reminded Erik of Santa Claus. The old man leaned over a book on a desk cluttered with notes and stacks of plant specimens. A bookcase graced the wall behind him.

"Erik," Gilbert said in his usual gruff voice. "Come in. Have a seat." He gestured toward a chair. "I'm sorry about the accident and your father," the old man said, lowering his voice. "He and I went back a long way."

An awkward silence hung between them for a moment before the words flowed from Erik. "I've been working with a friend, submitting to hypnosis to try and learn more about my past."

"I take it you've discovered something."

"I spoke in a weird language. I think I recognized the words, or at least what they meant. Some of them were botanical references."

Gilbert's bushy eyebrows raised. He rummaged through a drawer for a pencil and a pad. "Do you remember their names?"

"Something about a Vision Vine, a Sacred Cactus of Four Winds, a Holy Flower of the North Star, and the Flying Death."

Gilbert jotted down the names, speaking as he went. "Ayahuasca, Huachuma, and Datura, which the natives call Toé, and the Flying Death. Curare." He studied the pad and frowned. "That's a hell of a combination. Not one they would normally use together. It could be deadly."

"What can you tell me?"

"The Flying Death is curare. I'm sure you already know about it. It's used for arrow and blowgun darts by hunters in Central and South America. It inhibits the nicotinic acetylcholine receptor, which is a subtype of acetylcholine found at the neuromuscular junction causing weakness of the skeletal muscles, eventually causing death by asphyxiation due to paralysis of the diaphragm."

Gilbert selected a few books from the shelves behind him and set them on the table. Taking one off the top, he flipped through it until he found what he wanted. "Ayahuasca," he said, reading from the text. "The Vision Vine. Also known as Banisteriopsis, Caapi, Natema, Pindé, or Yajé. It grows in South America, especially in the Amazon region where we found you. It's one of the most potent hallucinogens in existence. The Indians believe it frees the soul to wander and return to the body at will. Ayahuasca means the 'vine of the soul' which refers to this freeing of the spirit. It's been growing in popularity in recent years because of reports extolling its so-called telepathic and healing powers."

Erik shook his head. "If that's true it would explain a few things." Like my animal contacts and my connection with that jaguar up in the mountains, he thought. "What's it do to you?"

"It usually induces nausea, dizziness, and vomiting, followed by a euphoric or aggressive state. The subject often sees overpowering attacks of huge snakes and jaguars."

Erik's heart jumped. "Snakes and jaguars?"

Gilbert stroked his beard. "The repetitiveness of snake and jaguar visions have intrigued psychologists. In many tribes the shaman becomes a feline during the intoxication, exercising his powers as a cat. They call it Otorongo."

Erik's stomach grew cold at the thought of his flight through the jungle. "A cat?"

Gilbert nodded. "Yekwana medicine men mimic the roars of jaguars and the souls of Peruvian Conibo-Shipibo shamans fly around in the form of birds. Among the Tukano, the partaker of Yajé feels himself pulled along by powerful winds. The Ecuadorian Zaparo also claim to experience a sensation of being lifted into the air."

Erik thought of the eagle. "And it has religious significance?"

"Spiritual significance would be a more apt descriptor. It's integral to the Yurupari ceremony of the Tukanoans; the basis of a man's tribal society and an adolescent male initiation rite."

Time to die as a boy. Become a man.

"The Tukanoans decorate the walls of their malocas with designs which can be traced to mythological beings seen in their visions," Gilbert continued. "Practically all the decorative elements in their culture are derived from hallucinatory imagery." He drew an odd looking picture of a human form and slid the pad over to Erik. "A recurring image in their designs is a man which portrays their ancestral spirit known as Master of the Animals."

Erik's heart raced faster as he studied the drawing. "Master of the Animals," he muttered. "What about the other plants?"

Gilbert closed his eyes and rubbed his temples. "Let me see. The Sacred Cactus of the Four Winds. That's San Pedro, otherwise known as Huachuma. It seems out of place here with Ayahuasca and Toé, which are jungle plants. It's a cactus that grows in the Andes and one of the most ancient of the magic plants of South America. Like peyote, it contains mescaline." He pulled another book from the pile and leafed through it. "The Indians say it is in tune with the powers of animals, strong personages, and beings of supernatural power. The evidence goes back to 1300 B.C." He flipped to a page, turned a book toward Erik and pointed to a picture of some pottery that depicted the cactus with jaguar and hummingbird figures.

"What does it do?"

"First it produces drowsiness and a dreamy state along with a feeling of lethargy, slight dizziness, then a great 'vision' and clearing of the faculties. A light numbness steals over the body, followed by tranquility, detachment, and a kind of visual force, inclusive of all the senses, including the telepathic sense of transmitting oneself across time and matter, like a removal of one's thought to a distant dimension. The Indians believe San Pedro was given to them by the gods to help them experience a separation of the soul from the body."

"And the third plant?"

"Datura. It's quite dangerous compared to the other two. Toé is not something to be trifled with. Its name comes from the dhatureas, bands of thieves in ancient India who used it to drug their victims. The Chibcha Indians of highland Colombia administered it to the wives and slaves of dead kings before burying them alive with their deceased masters. Sorcerers among the Yaqui of northern Mexico anoint their genitals, legs, and feet with a salve based on crushed Datura leaves to experience the sensation of flight and in medieval Europe witches rubbed their bodies with ointments made from belladonna, mandrake, and henbane. All relatives of Datura. Many women self-administered it through the moist tissues of their vaginas."

"Their what?"

Gilbert chuckled. "The witch's broomstick rides weren't through space, but across the hallucinatory landscape of their minds."

"And it's dangerous?"

"None of these plants should be taken lightly, especially Toé. In modest dosages it induces maddening hallucinations and delusions, followed by confusion, disorientation, and amnesia. An overdose can result in stupor and death."

"Do you think it could be connected to my amnesia?"

Gilbert scratched his beard and studied Erik. "The thought never crossed my mind before, but now that you mention it, when we found you near the Tukano, you were dressed like one and you were at the right age. You still wear that amulet?"

Erik pulled it from his shirt and held it out. "It's like American Express. Don't leave home without it. It's my good luck charm -- I think."

Gilbert fingered the amulet and nodded. "There's a possibility that Toé could be connected to your amnesia. More than any other drug, it's associated with the traditional moments of passage through the stages of birth, initiation, marriage, and death. Children of the Tubatulobal tribe drink it after puberty to 'obtain life'. After drinking large amounts, they fall into a stupor accompanied by hallucinations which last up to twenty-four hours. If an animal -- an eagle or a hawk, for example - is seen during the visions, it becomes the child's 'pet' or spiritual mascot for life. Children can never kill the animal they see in their Datura visions because these 'pets' can visit during serious illnesses and effect a cure."

You will meet your spirit animal and he will show you the path. Erik remembered the eagle that came to him in the delirium from his snakebite. Had it saved him?

"The Luiseño Indians of southern California believed that all youths had to undergo Datura narcosis during their puberty rites in order to become men," Gilbert said, breaking in on Erik's thoughts. "The Algonquin and other northeastern tribes used it, calling it wysoccan. At puberty, adolescent males were confined in special longhouses and for two or three weeks ate nothing but the drug. During the course of their extended intoxication, they forgot what it was to be a boy and learned what it meant to be a man."

The words from his session with Nicole filled his mind. *Time to die as a boy. Become a man.*

"The Jivaro in South America, headhunters of eastern Ecuador, give a potion called maikua to young boys at the age of six. They must seek their souls. If the boy is fortunate, his soul will appear to him in the form of a large pair of creatures, often animals such as jaguars or anacondas."

Erik saw the jaguar chasing him through the jungle. He remembered falling and looking up to see an anaconda, then he remembered the words he had uttered under hypnosis.

Behold the wonder of the sacred vision. The battle of the two sides of the spirit. You will meet your spirit animal and he will show you the path. He who has the vision is the brother of the sacred animal. The one who must lead.

There was a connection.

CHAPTER TWENTY

"You really think there's a connection to these plants?" Nicole looked wide-eyed at Erik, who sat across from her in a small candlelit booth tucked in the back of an Italian restaurant in La Jolla.

He nodded. "I know how strange it sounds, but think of everything I've told you and all I've experienced. There are too many parallels to ignore, especially when you consider how often the jaguar turns up."

Nicole rested her chin on her hand. "That part about the Master of the Animals is pretty wild."

"Everything fits, but I don't know where. I have to give it time to digest."

She put her hand on his. "If I hadn't seen what you can do, I'd say this was crazy, but in light of your abilities and background, or lack of it..." Her eyes glazed over, then came back into focus. "This goes against everything I've been trained to believe."

Erik gazed at the twin glitters of candlelight reflecting in her eyes.

"What are you going to do?" she said, breaking the spell.

He shrugged. "The smartest thing for now is to go with the flow. I know what I have a strong inclination to do, but I don't think I have all the information. Dr. Gilbert lent me some books. I'll check them out first."

"Erik?" Her hand tightened on his. "I know what you're thinking. You heard Dr. Gilbert. Those plants can be deadly. Promise me you won't do anything without me there to watch over you."

He looked in her eyes and saw the concern. A rush of emotion swept over him. He felt afraid and wished he could have met her under normal circumstances. He didn't want her to see his fear, so he forced a smile. "Promise."

The waitress came with their food and they ate in silence, stealing glances at one another. When they finished they took a ride down the coast, stopping at the beach in Del Mar near Torrey Pines where they sat together on the rocks watching moonlight reflecting off the waves while listening to the roar of water crashing on the shore. Erik studied her profile as the breeze ruffled her hair, then reached out and took her hand.

Later that night, he sat alone in bed poring over the books Dr. Gilbert had given him. In one of the sections on Ayahuasca he saw a picture of the Master of the Animals painted on the side of a Tukanoan Indian house and in some sand drawings. The pictures gave him the same feeling of nostalgia the ceremonial masks in the den did, only stronger.

On another page he saw a picture of two Indians preparing a brew. He read the caption beneath it.

> Among the Kofan of Colombia and Ecuador, medicine men prepare Curare and Yajé. There is an association between these two plant products. Yajé is taken before hunting in the belief that the visions will reveal the hiding places of the animals to be sought.

Curare. The Flying Death.

He let the thought sink in before rereading the caption. They believe the visions reveal the hiding places of the animals. How about a jaguar running rampant in the High Sierras? he thought.

He flipped through more pages, read about doses and methods of ingestion of the three plants. Different tribes used different plants combined in their own special mixtures. Most of them used a DMT containing plant with the Ayahuasca called Psychotria Viridis. The natives called it Chacruna.

The one that seemed out of place was the San Pedro cactus, known as Huachuma. It came from the mountains, not from the jungle like the other plants.

Pushing the books aside, he closed his eyes, trying to sort it all out. His thoughts jumped from one piece of information to the next, trying to fit them into a cohesive whole. A lot of it made sense, but much of it remained a mystery.

He turned off the light and tried to sleep, but his excitement kept him awake. After two hours, he sat up and went through the books again, reading everything he could find on the three plants. When he exhausted the literature, he studied the pictures, letting their familiarity fill his mind.

Two pictures held his interest more than the rest. Both from the ancient Chavin culture of Peru. One showed a ceramic vessel with a jaguar nestled among pieces of the San Pedro cactus; the other, an engraved stone from the Old Temple at Chavin de Huantar in the northern highlands of Peru.

The engraving showed the principal Chavin deity, an anthropomorphized creature with serpentine hair, jaguar fangs, and a belt of a double-headed serpent. In its eagle claws, it held a four-ribbed piece of San Pedro cactus. Four ribs were considered rare and very lucky, supposedly having special properties corresponding to the "four winds" and the "four roads", supernatural powers associated with the cardinal points.

The double-headed snake belt and serpentine hair reminded him of the cobra, the jaguar fangs of the cat that haunted him all his remembered life, and the claws of the eagle made him think of his protector, the magnificent bird that came to him in his delirium after the snakebite and soared above him as he came down from the summit of Mount Whitney. The creature seemed a key. And in its claws it held the cactus.

With these thoughts in his mind, he dozed…

…and felt himself gliding on the night breeze. In spite of the darkness, his vision came sharper. Below and around him he saw the outlines of the mountains in razor-sharp clarity. He hovered, enjoying the ease with which he stayed aloft, then tucked his wings in close and plummeted, thrilling at the speed with which he dropped.

The earth rushed toward him until a crash seemed imminent, then he spread his wings.

Swooping inches from the ground, he relished the intensity of each detail of the terrain. His momentum carried him back up until the wind caught him again, and with a few powerful beats of his wings, he soared once more, riding the breeze, diving again and again, duplicating his earlier feat, each thrill as satisfying as the last. The wind, the mountains, his heightened vision, sense of control and timing all felt natural, as if he belonged here. He watched smaller animals scurrying below him, darting from refuge to refuge, never staying long in the open.

Instinctively, he zeroed in on a field mouse, tracking its tiniest moves under the false shroud of darkness. He dropped lower, noiselessly riding the currents while the mouse continued its foraging, oblivious, then he swooped, catching it, hearing it squeal as his talons pierced its skin.

He carried it away to a mountaintop, where he ripped it apart with his beak and claws, savoring the warmth of the glistening strands of pink stringy meat.

The brutal act of hunting and tearing his quarry apart should have been unpleasant, but he acted from instinct.

His hunger sated, he took to the air again.

High up, he spied the first spark of morning sun shimmering on the horizon. His perception faded and with a feeling of sadness, he knew it was time to leave. Closing his eyes, he let go with his mind…

He awoke exhilarated, the experience fresh in his thoughts. Owl. Real. Immediate. The books lay spread around him on the bed. He picked them up and set them on the nightstand, then closed his eyes and relived the dream in vivid detail, from start to finish.

After calling Dr. Hoffelder, he went to the zoo and put in his first full day's work in weeks. Since his dream, he felt closer to them, as if he had been initiated into their world. Every time he thought of the dream, he caught himself smiling.

In the weeks that followed, Erik fell into a routine of hard work at UCSD and at the zoo. He and Nicole met every night for dinner and sometimes a movie, never going beyond holding hands, an occasional hug, and a rare kiss on the cheek.

The regularity of his schedule seemed to reinforce something. Not only was his life settling into an agreeable pattern, but so were his dreams. Each night he dreamed of being a different animal, but he had no control over what he would experience.

More often than not, he soared as an eagle.

CHAPTER TWENTY ONE

Erik stood at the edge of a mountain meadow, his sight and hearing vigilant. The light breeze and gentle caress of the morning sun felt good on his back. A feeling of oneness filled his heart as he watched a doe and its fawn grazing. Satisfied they were safe, he went back to the sweet-tasting leaves and twigs of manzanita he'd been eating, savoring the taste of the different bushes and plants, thrilled at the ease with which he could cross a meadow with a few leaps.

He bounded further up the slope, stopping to listen and sniff the air for danger. He checked the doe and fawn again. Except for an underlying sense of apprehension, being a deer felt natural.

The wind shifted and his head shot up catching a scent. Danger. He remained rigid. Listening. Trembling. He caught a flurry of movement as the doe and fawn vaulted into the safety of the forest. Nothing else moved, but the threatening scent remained strong. He strained to hear something more. Only the sound of the wind came to him. The meadow had been swallowed up in an ominous silence.

The brush to his left came alive in a blur of light brown fury as a snarling mountain lion leaped toward him.

A flood of adrenaline made his legs spring as though touched by a live wire. The cat swiftly closed the gap, bearing down. Heart racing, frantic, Erik leaped and zig-zagged. The mountain lion growled, Erik cut to the right, it followed, he cut back, and it pounced. Twin agonies of white-hot pain shot through him. Claws buried in his flanks, followed by the weight of the cat. Pain crushed him, teeth pierced his neck, and he stumbled, feeling the warm flow of life jetting from his body, cutting him down. He struggled to stand while pain knifed through him again and again. His vision blurred, his head fell back, giving him a brief view of the blue sky, then fangs ripped at his throat and darkness closed in…

Erik's eyes flew open. He stared up at the ceiling, heart pounding. His throat felt dry, his breathing heavy. His arms and legs had tangled in the sheets. He put his hand to his chest and took a deep breath. "Whew!"

He experienced the roles of predator and prey with a deeper understanding, shuddering at the thought of the claws and fangs that brought his dream to an end.

In the weeks following his new discoveries, Erik worked closely with Fritz Hoffelder, probing the mental and emotional state of animals, "feeling" their thoughts, while Hoffelder concentrated on their physical condition. When an animal became sick or injured, instead of darts and hypodermics, Erik calmed them and gave them an oral sedative.

He told Hoffelder about his dreams one morning as the two men worked on a drugged flamingo with an injured leg.

"I've been both predator and prey," he said as Hoffelder completed a suture. "Both are exciting, but I'd much rather be the hunter."

"I imagine it's quite terrifying to be a victim."

"That's the downside, but the experience does give me more insight. I wish I could choose which animals to experience. I never know what I'm going to be."

Hoffelder looked up. "Have you ever really tried?"

"What do you mean?"

"Make a conscious effort to pick the animal you want to dream. Assert yourself instead of allowing it to control you. Before you go to sleep at night, try to picture an animal and keep the thought of it firmly in your mind."

"I don't think I can."

Hoffelder bent back to his work. "Why not?"

Erik thought about it. Why hadn't he tried? "I don't know," he blurted. "There's really no reason."

"Good." Hoffelder chuckled. "Let me know what happens."

Erik smiled, realizing for the first time how much Fritz had prodded him into expanding the range of his experience. "I'll do that." He held the flamingo's leg straight while Fritz bandaged it.

"Speaking of asserting yourself, how is it going with your charming lady friend?"

"I'll be seeing her tonight."

"Be sure to give her my regards."

When they finished with the bird, Fritz took it to a holding cell in the complex and Erik went upstairs to call Nicole. She picked up on the second ring.

"Hey, beautiful, it's me. Can I see you tonight?"

"It's nice to hear your voice. It's been a busy morning. I haven't had much chance to think about anything."

"I don't know about you, but I'm getting tired of eating out. Why don't you come over to my place tonight?"

She hesitated, then said, "You're going to cook?"

Now Erik hesitated. "Yeah, yeah, I'll cook, but you'll be sorry."

She giggled. "I don't think so. What time?"

"Seven-thirty."

He left work early, stopped at the store for groceries and hurried home to clean the house. For dinner he made Fettuccine Alfredo and set the table with a linen cloth and two candles. He put soft jazz on the stereo, dimmed the lights and lit the candles when he heard her knock.

"Hi," she said when he opened the door. She came in and looked around. "Nice place." She pulled a bouquet from behind her back and gave him a hug.

"For me? I never had anyone give me flowers. Come on." He gestured toward the kitchen.

She followed him. "Smells good. And candles. Romantic."

He pulled a vase down from the cupboard and she arranged the flowers. He gave her a quick tour of the house before sitting down to dinner.

He studied her as they ate, wondering what it would be like to hold her close. Her soft lips on his. Would she be offended if he kissed her?

After dinner, he took her into the den and sat next to her on the couch. "This is my favorite room." He pointed to the artifacts on the walls. "This is probably going to sound strange, but those things make me comfortable." He sighed. "Dad and I spent a lot of time in here talking."

She kicked her shoes off and curled up on the couch, resting her head on his chest. "It's hard for you without him, isn't it?"

Erik closed his eyes. "It's not so bad if I keep busy, but when I'm by myself it gets lonely. Having you in my life is a blessing. I don't know what I'd do if you left."

She looked up at him and smiled. "I'm not planning on it, unless you chase me off."

"No way." He leaned over and pressed his mouth to hers. She parted her lips for their first kiss and their tongues touched, mingling in a delicate exchange of affection.

CHAPTER TWENTY TWO

Not wanting to rush things, Erik only kissed Nicole. After she left, he went to bed fantasizing what it would be like to make love to her, but as he drifted off to sleep his warm thoughts of her flitted away, replaced by the voice of Dr. Hoffelder.

"Try to pick an animal and keep the thought of it firmly in your mind."

He started awake. What animal would he like to be? Turning on to his side, he looked out his window and glimpsed something flitting past a street light. A bat.

Closing his eyes, he rolled onto his back and fixed the image of a bat in his mind, visualizing its habitat, and imagining what it would be like to be one...

... Opening his eyes to damp darkness. He hung upside down, sensing others hanging close. He blinked, allowing his eyes to adjust, but they didn't function well.

His excitement brought a high-pitched note of pleasure from him that bounced off the floor and walls of the cave, giving him a clearer image of his surroundings that more than made up for his diminished sight.

He let go with his claws and dropped, spreading his delicate wings like a kite, flitting through the cave, navigating its narrow passages by letting out short cries that echoed back to him, guiding him out into the clear night sky. As a bird he had to maintain his flying speed in order to stay aloft, but these thin, kitelike batwings allowed him to hover, stop and turn with astonishing precision.

Uttering a short burst of sound, his sensitive ears "saw" a moth fluttering ahead. He zeroed in on it and made a quick cut, catching it unaware before flying off in search of more. When he became thirsty, he found a small pond. Dipping low over the surface, he scooped water into his mouth as he skimmed along the top.

He hunted and ate his way through the night, enjoying himself between meals by exploring the high-speed acrobatics his agility provided him.

When his light-sensitive eyes caught the first indications of the approaching day, he flew back to the dark safety of his cave to find a comfortable spot on the ceiling...

Waking in the predawn gray of his bedroom he sat up, playing back the experience in his mind, then threw back the covers, hopped out of bed, and drove to the zoo early. After checking with security he went to the tiger pit, hopped down, and played with the cat before anybody could see him, then he walked back to the compound, spending time with all the animals, except the snakes. He shuddered at the thought of touching the mind of a cold-blooded reptile, let alone dreaming of being one. Good thing his nightly excursions hadn't taken him in that direction. As for birds and mammals, he made a mental note to dream of being each one as he touched their minds.

He found Dr. Hoffelder at the office hunched over some of Phineas's old texts. For the first time, Erik noticed that the room had taken on the personality of its new occupant. A bookshelf full of veterinary texts on one wall, a cuckoo clock from the Black Forest, travel posters from Berlin and Hamburg on another, and a glass cabinet full of beer steins. He felt a twinge of longing for Phineas.

"I picked a bat," he said, not wanting to dwell on his loss.

Hoffelder looked up, his bushy eyebrows moving toward his bulbous nose, then he beamed, sending them in the other direction. "*Der fledermaus.* You dreamed it. That's wonderful. I had a feeling you'd be able to do it. What was it like?"

Erik pulled up a chair and relayed his hunting and flying experiences, stressing how strange it was to utter sounds and following the echoes with his "radar." Fritz listened carefully, his head resting on his hand. When Erik finished, the older man made no response. A distant look filled his eyes.

"What are you thinking about?" Erik asked.

Fritz looked up wide-eyed, then his thin hands danced through the air. "I was thinking what a valuable tool this could be. When we wish to do an in-depth study of an animal's lifestyle, your dreams can give us great insight into its habits."

"I do feel a deeper understanding of each of the animals I've dreamed."

"Something else has crossed my mind too," Fritz said, lowering his voice.

"What's that?"

"Your nightmares with the jaguar. If you can control what animal you dream about, then I would assume those bad dreams are over."

Erik kicked his feet up on the desk and put his hands behind his head. "Hadn't thought about that, but the dreams I had about him were different. Not like the other animals."

"How so?"

Erik put his feet down and leaned forward. "It's like I'm inside and outside of him at the same time; both participant and observer. I didn't want to be there. It felt like something held me against my will."

"You had no control then. Maybe now things will be different."

"Maybe. Then again, maybe not."

That night he went to Nicole's, finding her waiting at the door in jeans and a teal silk blouse with the top two buttons open. The smell of her perfume made him giddy. She surprised him with a kiss that was both tender and passionate. Her lips felt as smooth as the material of her blouse.

"I've been thinking about you since I left last night," she said. "I've purposely held back getting involved with you. It violates the sanctity of a healthy doctor patient relationship, but in light of your remarkable abilities my thinking has shifted from that of doctor patient to colleagues exploring a brave new world of research."

"If this is the greeting I get, you need to do a lot more thinking."

"I don't think so." She smiled and took his hand, leading him to a small overstuffed couch in one corner of her apartment.

"Listen," Erik said, resting his hand on her knee. "I know this is going to sound weird, and believe me, I don't want to spoil the mood, but do you think you can hypnotize me?"

Mild shock registered on her face, then she regained her composure. "Now?"

He told her about dreaming of being a bat and how he could dream of any animal he chose, then he told her Fritz's ideas about the jaguar nightmares.

"If I can control things," he said, patting her knee, "I want some reassurance that the dreams *are* over. Besides it's been awhile since you put me under."

She bit her lower lip, then took his hands in hers. "Let me get my notebook and recorder."

He came to an hour later, slumped back on the couch, Nicole sitting in the armchair next to him.

"All we got were the animal cries," she said. "I tried to push you past it, but -- nothing. I even asked about the jaguar. You became frightened and wouldn't say anything. I didn't think it wise to push it. I'm sorry."

He made a dismissive gesture. "I wanted to give it a try. It looks like it's going to take a bigger jolt to get past whatever's blocking me. I think the plants are the only way."

"You know how I feel about that."

He sighed. "Yeah, I know. Enough of this."

He reached over, grabbed her by the wrists and pulled her on top of him. She giggled when he wrapped his arms around her. When he kissed her on the neck, she pulled away and they studied each other, their eyes communicating their feelings better than words.

She stroked his hair. "Erik," she whispered.

He pulled her closer. Their lips touched, then pressed together, her softness yielding to him, his tongue meeting hers in a tender ballet.

He ran his hands down her sides and worked them up under her blouse, marveling at her curves and the softness of her body. She shivered when his hands touched her bare skin. She felt good. Warm.

Taking him by the hand, she led him to her bedroom where they fell on the bed, entwined, then she rolled over on top of him and unbuttoned her blouse. He kissed her on the neck and undid her bra, trailing wet kisses to her breasts until she arched her back and let out a soft moan. Her tongue darted hungrily into his mouth as they shed their clothes, then danced lightly about his ear. "I love you," she whispered.

The warmth of her moist breath sent a thrill coursing through him. "You know how much I love you." He kissed her neck, her ears, and her eyelids, his urgency building until he could contain himself no more.

CHAPTER TWENTY THREE

L ater that night, Erik lay awake, Nicole cuddled beside him, her head resting on his chest. "What are you going to do?" She said after a long silence.

"I don't know. There's nothing I'd like more than to be normal. I still can't remember my past, but nothing else has happened. I'm in control of my dreams and haven't been bothered by the jaguar, but I know I'm connected with it. I'm hoping that it might be gone, but..."

She looked up at him. "What if something else happens?"

"I'll deal with it when it comes. That's all I can do."

"And what if nothing happens? Are you going to be happy not knowing your past?"

Erik sighed. "Hypnosis has taken us as far as it's going to. I need to do something drastic to send a wake-up call to my brain."

"You've been thinking about those plants, haven't you?"

He put his arms around her and squeezed. "Sure, I've been thinking about it, but I have to be honest, I'm scared."

"You don't *have* to do it, you know."

"I don't have to do anything, but I'm more afraid of not knowing my past than I am of those plants." He shook his head. "All I want is to lead a life that's quiet and as close to normal as possible. With you."

She kissed him on the chest, then closed her eyes. A few minutes later her breathing came low and steady. As Erik drifted off to sleep, he heard the hoot of an owl...

He knew he had become one again when the image of the night forest came into sharp definition. Spreading his wings, he took flight until his vision blurred like a camera gone out of focus. He fought to keep his perception, but his mind drifted like a radio losing the reception of a weak station while a stronger one exerted its power.

The force pulled him to another place, making his awareness shift and adjust to a new point of reference. Low to the ground. His vision refocused, sharper than it had been moments before.

He had a keen sense of smell and a feeling of brutal power in his four limbs, along with a strange dichotomy; part of this beast, yet removed, floating along with it, both participant and observer. He remembered this feeling from his nightmares. No control.

Equal parts fascination and fear held him as he braced himself for the night's adventure. He had no choice but to participate in whatever happened. He could only watch, helpless to act -- at the mercy of his host.

Otorongo.

He sniffed the night air, sorting through the myriad scents, searching for the prey he savored most. He smelled two or three smaller creatures, but ignored them. He longed for the soft, hairless flesh of a human.

Crossing a ridge, he bounded down a rocky embankment until he came to a trail where he stopped and sniffed. The scent of humans lingered. He broke into a trot, following the trail until he caught the telltale, acrid smell of campfires, then the sound of voices carrying on the night wind. He spotted three fires at the top of a hill. Two close together and one further off. He skirted the first two and closed in on the last one. Three figures stood around it. Hunkering close to the ground, he crept toward them on his belly.

Erik wanted to scream, but the force held him. He could only watch and experience.

He craned his neck and raised his nose until he picked up their scents mingled with the smell of fire. All male. Not as sweet and tender as that of females, but satisfying all the same. He paused, listening as their movements and voices changed.

"I've got to take a piss," the one with the strongest scent called back, leaving his companions.

The beam of a flashlight came straight for him, passing within inches of his head.

He crouched lower, muscles bunching, senses poised. The silhouette of a heavy-set man came within five feet, then stopped, relieving himself in the bushes. The acrid scent of human urine made his eyes water. When the man finished and turned away, he pounced, knocking the man to the ground. The flashlight winked out.

The man gave a short, startled cry that cut short as the jaguar bore down on him. Hands flailed. Fists beat ineffectively. A face, frozen in wide-eyed terror. Massive jaws sank into the soft flesh of the throat. Ecstasy as hot blood jetted into his mouth, filling him with warmth. A ragged scream turned into a liquid gurgle. The body spasmed, then subsided to a mindless twitch.

"Did you hear something?" one of the voices said, breaking in on the frenzy. "Shit! What's he doing now?"

The cat froze, blood oozing from its jaw.

"Quit fucking around!" the other voice said. Then, "He's just doing that stupid bear routine again."

Erik studied the lifeless form beneath him, then peered at the other two huddled near the fire. Grasping his victim by the meat of the shoulder, he dragged him behind a rock, then circled the campfire until he perched on a log behind the other two men.

"What the hell's he doing out there?" the taller one said.

"Goddamn Hank. Always fucking around."

"Maybe I better go check on him. Hank's an idiot, but he might've fallen and hurt himself."

"Want me to go with you?"

"No, that's all right." The man rose and disappeared into the darkness on the other side of the clearing.

The jaguar cleared the space between him and the man on the log in three leaps, knocking his victim to the ground with all his weight. Something cracked and the man grunted.

A sickening numbness enveloped Erik like a protective shield.

The cat swatted with his paw, raking the man's face and throat, slicing an eyeball, turning it into a mass of darkened crimson that glistened in the firelight. The other eye stared wildly up at him. The mouth moved. No sound. He raked again and again, then bit at the throat, once more savoring hot saltiness. Fingers clutched at emptiness as though trying to hold on to life as it slipped away.

He heard a gasp, looked up from his kill and saw a tall man staring in disbelief, hand to his mouth. A low growl issued from somewhere within. The man backed away, then turned and ran. The cat sprang, smelling the waves of fear radiating from the fleeing man.

He closed the gap in seconds and pounced, paws catching his quarry at the back of his legs, slicing through the hamstrings. The man stumbled forward, screaming.

The high-pitch of his cry drove the jaguar's excitement to its zenith. He leaped onto the man's back and flipped him over with his paw.

"Please," the man begged. "Please God! Don't kill me!"

The cat batted the man's face with his paw, claws sheathed, then batted again like a kitten playing with catnip.

"P-Please God," he sobbed. "Let me live."

The man's head jerked to the side, his cries now moans. The jaguar snarled, pummeled the head and fastened his jaws on the exposed throat, savagely shaking the limp form from side to side, severing the head from the body.

Blackness pumped from the stump on the shoulders jolting Erik more than anything else he'd seen. A fuzzy gray enveloped him. He went toward it, throwing his mind into the only escape available...

...and woke up in bed, thrashing. His stomach writhed, then heaved. Sobs wracked him. Tears ran down his face. He took in his surroundings and breathed in a deep tremulous sob.

Nicole stared back at him, wide-eyed. "What is it?" She whispered.

CHAPTER TWENTY FOUR

Erik sat in his office at the zoo, staring at his computer, unable to work and unable to think. His head pulsed with sharp stabbing pain while his mind played back the horrifying details of the massacre.

"You came in early," Fritz said from behind him.

Erik jumped, sending a cup of coffee flying.

"Sorry." He picked up the cup. "You startled me." He pushed himself back from the desk, and cleaned up the mess. He felt Fritz studying him as he finished.

"Why don't you go home and get some rest?" Fritz said. "You have me worried."

"Did I ever tell you about the dreams I've been having of being a jaguar that kills campers in the mountains?"

"You dreamed it?"

Erik nodded.

"And you think the rangers will call you today?"

"Bet on it."

As if on cue Erik's cell phone rang. He snatched it up, saw Mitchell's number displayed and braced himself, trying to sound relaxed. "Hi, Scott. What's up?"

"He's hit again," Mitchell said, sounding grim.

"The jag?"

The line went silent. For a moment Erik had the crazy thought that Mitchell had figured out his connection with the jaguar, then "I think there might be more than one cat."

Erik flashed on the three mauled bodies. "What makes you say that?" The phone felt slippery in his hand.

"Three bodies this time. All men. One of them decapitated."

"Where?"

"Sequoia National Park. Bearpaw Meadow."

What can I say? Erik thought. Hey, Scott, I tried to be an owl, but this feeling came over me and I had to hunt. I was there when it happened. Trapped inside the jaguar. I took part in the murders. Hell, I experienced everything the jag did, but not consciously. I mean I was conscious, but I watched while he did it.

"Erik?"

"Huh? Oh, sorry. Just trying to piece it together. This behavior is far from characteristic. We're dealing with a disturbed animal. Or animals. I know this sounds strange, but I think it's only one jag. You sending a chopper?"

"Should be at Lindbergh in a couple of hours. I appreciate you coming up. We really need you on this one."

"I'm as interested in stopping this as you are. I'll meet you up there."

The copter dropped Erik in front of the Bearpaw Meadow Ranger Station under strong winds and a leaden sky. A grim-faced Mitchell met him and handed him a Colt .45 and holster. "Strap it on. Orders from the mucky-mucks in Washington. No one involved in this investigation goes unarmed."

Erik followed Mitchell down to the campsite. The moment he saw it, his legs felt rubbery. The scene looked different from the one at Big Pine. More rangers and this time National Guardsmen. Some had sidearms like his and Mitchell's, but most carried pump shotguns; a few had high-powered hunting rifles with scopes. Others toted high-powered assault weapons. Twice as many federal officials in suits milled about than at Big Pine. Three of them approached Erik and Scott.

"Washington's breathing down our necks on this one," Mitchell said, as if reading Erik's thoughts. "Five dead now. They've given us a thirty man task force. They want results."

"We'll see what we can do."

Mitchell introduced Erik to the three men. The ranking official's name was Schmitten, a lanky dark-haired man with cold, gray eyes and a neatly-trimmed mustache who looked to be somewhere in his fifties.

"We've gone over this area with a fine-toothed comb," Schmitten said.

Erik made a show of studying the terrain.

"That doesn't mean anything." Scott squeezed Erik's shoulder. "My man here is a regular Daniel Boone. I'll bet dollars to doughnuts, he comes up with more than your guys."

Erik cringed inwardly, feeling undeserving of the praise. Mitchell's words drove pangs of guilt into him like a spike.

"Our forensics man says the maulings occurred within the last twelve hours." Schmitten pointed to three body bags laid out alongside one another. "We kept them here so you could get a look at the wounds." He jabbed a thumb over his shoulder. "And we have a witness who found the first body."

Erik saw a man, a woman, and two rangers sitting with a small blond-haired boy wrapped in a blanket, staring straight ahead. Erik felt bad for the youngster. "No need to talk to him," he heard himself say. "Get him to somebody for counseling."

Schmitten turned and called to one of the men. "Hey, Stebel, get the kid down to a doctor."

Erik's stomach rolled when he thought about what he'd see in the body bags. He had no reason to look at the bodies, but these men didn't know that. He had to make it look as if his findings came from logical reasoning. Logic, he thought. That's a novelty. He decided to put it off. "If you don't mind," he said. "I'd like to survey the surroundings first. It's going to be hard enough trying to track him with the wind and all these people stomping around."

Schmitten looked to Mitchell who nodded. "Sure," he said. "A little time isn't going to make much of a difference. Those guys aren't in a hurry to go anywhere."

Erik gritted his teeth. "Okay," he said, fighting back his anger. He looked at the blackened dirt by the campfire, then circled the campsite, finally pointing behind the log to a spot where the grass was barely matted. "He crouched here and waited to strike. Probably took one man off by himself, then waited for the other two to separate." He followed the path he had taken the night before, spotted a track and pointed. "Here's a paw print. Get a man on it."

"Damn," Schmitten said.

Mitchell hushed him. "Let him do his thing. He'll fill us in as he goes."

Erik walked to the spot where the jag had downed the first man and pointed. "He came in this way." He led Mitchell and Schmitten to the trail and followed it, pointing to tracks from time to time and marking them for casts to be taken. After going a couple of miles, he pointed up an embankment. "He came down from there. That's where you want to direct a search, but I'd be careful. Keep your men in groups of three."

Schmitten cleared his throat. "Just a minute. I'm the one…"

"Who's going to be responsible if that jag makes another meal out of one of your men? Make no mistake about it, Mr. Schmitten." He bent over and pointed to a tiny shred of reddened flannel. "Once you head up there, you're on his turf." He turned to Mitchell. "Sorry. No fur samples this time. I don't know if this is any comfort, but there's definitely only one animal." He swallowed hard. "Let's go take a look at the remains so we can get them out of here."

Schmitten picked up the bloodied bit of flannel with a pair of tweezers, and the three men walked back to the campsite.

Erik gagged when he saw the torn out throat of the first corpse. The man's face swam into view. He recognized it from last night. Dried, crusted blood congealed on the man's chest and shoulders. His arms were bent at odd angles. Erik pointed to the bloody paw prints and bite marks on the man's chest and arms, then turned to Mitchell and Schmitten. "Panthera Onca. Same as the samples we took earlier."

Schmitten leaned over and studied the body, then looked at Mitchell. "You're right. He is sharp."

Erik's stomach did a flip-flop. "Let's see the other two and get this over with."

The second man also had a chunk torn out of his neck. The empty eye socket had become a blackened mass of clotted blood. The remaining eye stared accusingly up at him. Erik's thoughts flashed to the previous night. The eye glistening in the firelight. Claws slashing. He shuddered, then pointed to the slices and fang punctures on the man's face and neck. "That fits the pattern of a jag's kill."

He moved to the third one. The severed head lay close to the body, but with nothing to support it, it tilted off at a gruesome angle. The area around the face looked bruised and puffy. The mouth open. *Please God. Please don't let him kill me. P-Please. Let me live.*

Erik's chest tightened. A rush of saliva filled his mouth. He stumbled aside and vomited.

"Can't blame you," Schmitten said. "Something like this is hard to take."

CHAPTER TWENTY FIVE

After a grueling day in the mountains and a non-stop session at the zoo backing up his claims with hard evidence, Erik drove home, ready to collapse. The hammering in his head had settled into an agonizing pressure behind his eyes. All emotion had been wrung from his body while his mind raced in a futile attempt to escape the inevitable truth.

He had conflicting feelings when he saw Nicole's car in the driveway. Part of him felt thankful for her being there, someone to comfort him and ease his pain. Another part felt ashamed, not wanting to face her.

He parked and rested his head on the steering wheel. He had to tell her the truth, but what would she think? He couldn't bear the thought of her abandoning him. He looked up and saw her in the doorway. Gritting his teeth against the pain crashing through his head, he climbed out of the car.

"Erik!" She said when she saw him. "You look terrible. Are you all right?"

He winced at the shock on her face. She hugged him, and stroked his hair. Her tenderness made his throat feel tight. He felt like crying, but kept control.

"What happened up there?"

"Three murders," he mumbled. "Bloody. Senseless."

She took his briefcase, set it aside, and led him into the den where she took his shoes off and made him lie on the couch. It felt awkward having a woman fuss over him, but more than that, he felt undeserving. He pressed his palms into his eyes.

"Headache?"

He nodded. "Can't think straight right now. Head hurts."

She kissed him on the forehead. "Come on." She helped him up from the couch and took him to his bedroom where she undressed him and tucked him in. "Sleep," she whispered, crawling into bed beside him. "We'll talk later."

He wanted to say something, but felt emotionally numb. After kissing her on the cheek, he turned over and escaped into sleep.

His headache greeted him the next morning, but his stomach had settled. He felt weak and hunger gnawed at him. He turned and saw Nicole asleep beside him, fully clothed. Couldn't ask for a prettier guardian angel, he thought.

She opened her eyes, smiled, and kissed him lightly. "Feeling better?"

He sat up with his back against the headboard and rubbed his eyes. The movement made his head throb. "A little." He glanced at the clock on the night stand. "Shouldn't you be at your office?"

She propped her head up on her hand. "You had me worried sick. I wasn't about to leave you." She sat up and put her arms around her knees. "You've had a bad time and you need someone. I'm here."

He rubbed his head, then reached over and took her into his arms. "Thanks, babe."

She squeezed him. "Go jump in the shower. It'll make you feel better. I'll fix something to eat, then we'll talk."

The events of the last couple of days rushed into his mind as if some hidden floodgate had opened. His guilt rode the crest of the wave. "I'm not sure I'm ready."

"I won't force you, but you have to trust someone, and if you can't trust me, then -- well -- dammit, Erik, whether you like it or not, we're in this together." He heard the conviction in her voice, but her blazing eyes said it even more. Not telling her would be a mistake.

He showered, took three aspirin, and followed the smell of fresh coffee and pancakes. Nicole studied him in silence while he ate.

When he finished, she took him by the hand, led him to the den, and pushed him down in the recliner. She stretched out on the couch, coffee cup in hand. "I want it all, from the beginning."

He looked at her, his eyes searching hers. "The killings?"

"Yes."

"I know who the murderer is." He watched her face.

A tiny frown creased her brow. "The jaguar that's loose in the mountains, right?"

"Technically you're correct, but he's not responsible." His mouth went dry.

The crease in her brow grew deeper. "If he's not responsible, then who or what is?"

Erik stared back without answering. He looked down at his hands, unable to look at her any more. "I dreamed the first murder. The two lovers up at Big Pine. I didn't know what was happening. That's when I went to you. Then the other things -- my Dad's death -- something happened inside me. We had that session and I learned about the plants. Then I began dreaming of being different animals. At first I couldn't control what animals I dreamed about, then I could. I gained control and picked the animals I wanted to dream. Now this."

The blood had drained from her face. "I don't understand."

"I'm not just dreaming. I'm *becoming* these animals. Going into their bodies. It's real. Not dreams. I dreamed myself into that jaguar. The phone call came the next day, just like last time. I don't have control over this -- this weird thing I do. I didn't want to be with that jaguar, but there was nothing I could do. I tried to get away, tried to stop it -- something forced me to participate in the killing. The rangers up there think I'm some kind of wunderkind. I'm not. I'm a murderer."

She held up her hand. "Hold it right there. You're taking responsibility for something you admit you were unable to control. That's like waking up in the back seat of a car and realizing the driver is drunk before you can do anything to avoid an accident. Are you responsible?"

Erik stared at the floor. "I'm connected to that Jaguar."

"How can you be so sure?"

"I think I can prove it, but I need help."

She leaned toward him. "What kind of help?"

A chill skittered over his scalp as he spoke. "I need to give my brain a jolt. See if I can break loose whatever's hiding in there."

"Those plants?"

He nodded. "I have to get control of my ability. Once I do, I'm sure the killing will end."

CHAPTER TWENTY SIX

E rik and Nicole sat in his kitchen studying the woody pieces of Ayahuasca vine Dr. Gilbert had given him.

"According to the doc," Erik said. "The natives prefer the bark from younger stems. They're supposed to produce different effects than the older ones."

Nicole leaned over for a closer look. "It's amazing to think such an innocent looking plant can do so much."

Erik picked up a piece of the knotty looking vine and examined it closely. "I think I recognize it."

"You sure you want to go through with this?"

"You sure you want to watch?"

"I'm against it, but I know how much you want to get to the bottom of all this craziness. I'm not going to let you do it alone. I'll watch and record whatever happens and if I think you're in trouble, I'm rushing you to Scripps."

"Let's see what we can do."

Following the directions from one of Doctor Gilbert's books, Erik scraped the bark from the stem and boiled it until a thick, strong-smelling liquid remained.

"I'm supposed to take it in small doses," he said, sniffing the brackish mixture.

"Let's go in the den," Nicole said. "You feel the most comfortable there."

He followed her into the den, holding the pot in front of him. "I'll take a shot glass full every fifteen minutes, up to an hour, if I have to. If I get too weird, I'm counting on you to take it from me."

"If I had my way, I'd take it away from you now."

He set the pot down and gave her a kiss. "Thanks for watching over me." He settled in his recliner and took the first shot, gagging as the bitter fluid went down. "Ugh!" He chased it with a sip of root beer. "Nasty."

Fifteen minutes later he did it again.

After the third shot, he felt nauseous, then giddy and nervous. Sweat poured from him. "I think I've had enough." A vortex of dizziness swallowed him. He rushed to the bathroom and vomited, then diarrhea set in. When he felt as if his body had nothing left to give, he came back to the chair and closed his eyes.

"What's happening?" Nicole asked.

A euphoric feeling set in. "I feel good. Seeing light. Mainly white. But changing. Hazy. Smoky blue."

Swirls of smoky light played across his mind like colored searchlights through fog. He felt relaxed and at peace, yet highly aware. The intensity of the lights increased, drawing him toward them. He heard Nicole's disembodied voice, but it didn't come from any particular direction so he let it blend with the rest of his surroundings and flowed toward the lights.

He thought he might be in the jungle, only it felt different. Vivid, yet too real, making it unreal. The mists swayed in a gentle rhythm, then parted, leaving him face to face with a massive, emerald-eyed jaguar.

Otorongo.

He tried to scream. Tried to run. His legs didn't respond. The jaguar snarled and leaped. Its maw closed on his head, then passed through him. The jungle melted and the lights returned, then dimmed. He drifted, slipping somewhere between what felt like sleep and dreaming.

His pulse boomed in his ears, matching the thump of his heart. The rhythm. The beat. He knew it. The wind gusted, first blowing past, then pulling him toward the drums.

The jungle. Indians. He knew this place. The big house made out of trees. The maloca. The drums boomed deeper. Other men surrounded him. Indians. He looked at the dark-skinned boy next to him. His brother? An older man spoke and the women scattered to the surrounding forest.

They can hear the horns but to look upon them is death.

Four pairs of horns were pulled from hiding places. The players sat in a semi-circle and played the first low mournful notes. Older men opened boxes and produced brilliant feather ruffs that they tied to the mid-section of the longer horns.

Four men with perfect rhythm danced through the maloca, blowing the newly decorated horns, advancing and retreating with short steps. Two of them danced out the door, horns raised to the sky, then returned. The expanding and contracting feather ruffs shot a beautiful burst of translucent color against the stronger light.

Father appeared dressed in red with a strangely shaped clay jar. An amber claw and tooth amulet hung prominently on his chest. Someone served tiny round gourds full of a thick brown bitter liquid. The boy next to him vomited. Erik felt sick himself, but held it in. The volume diminished and father remained in the center of the maloca, bowing, advancing, and retreating.

The older men outfitted themselves with headbands resplendent with guacamayo feathers, tall feathery egret plumes, oval pieces of the russet skin of the howler monkey, armadillo hide disks, loops of monkey-hair cord, quartzite cylinders, and jaguar tooth belts. Forming a swaying, dancing semi-circle, each man put his right hand on his neighbor's shoulder and they all shifted and stamped in unison. Father led, blowing smoke on his companions from a big cigar held in an engraved ceremonial fork. His long, polished rattle-lance vibrated constantly.

The group chanted familiar sounds, their voices rising and falling, mingling with the mysterious booming tones of the horns. Father's voice rose above them all.

"Behold the wonder of the sacred vision. The battle of the two sides of the spirit. You will meet your spirit animal and he will show you the path. He who has the vision is the brother of the sacred animal. The one who must lead the people in his thirtieth season."

Erik's vision grew hazy. A flurry of colors. He looked over at the boy next to him and caught an angry glare. A shiver ran through him, then he drifted with a wind that carried him up out of the maloca and over the trees, leaving him somewhere in the forest.

He saw the jaguar prowling and froze, his heart fluttering against his ribs. The cat's gaze held him. Angry. Malevolent. Like the Indian boy's.

He sighed, relieved when the cat slunk away, then an anaconda dropped from a branch above, its head inches from his face. Fear gripped him, but he felt more afraid of giving in to it. The snake opened its mouth as if to swallow him. He felt compelled to give himself to it, but something stopped him. To do so would be a mistake. The sacred animal must lead. Show him the path.

The serpent drew back, eyes glittering like sunlight off the surface of a gem, opening its mouth again. He wanted to give himself. Wanted to free himself. He closed his eyes.

When he opened them, his breath caught and his legs buckled. A cobra reared back, neck hooded, ready to strike. He knew if he gave in, it wouldn't strike. He closed his eyes again. He would not be forced. He had to choose. He could choose.

A fluttering sound came from far away. A flapping. He opened his eyes again. The fluttering filled his vision and the eagle swooped down out of the trees, catching the serpent in its beak, then rising, taking the writhing snake high above the forest.

Erik's heart soared with the eagle and in a flash he *became* the eagle, gliding on the winds, a snake in his beak, first an anaconda, then a cobra. The serpent struck at him. He flipped sideways. It missed. It struck out again. He dodged and felt fear, but he sensed power in the eagle's form.

The snake changed again. Now an anaconda wrapping around him, pinning his wings until he plummeted. He bit deep, his claws digging at the cold skin of his antagonist. The snake squeezed more. He fell faster. The ground flew toward him. At the last moment, the snake loosened its grip and Erik spread his wings, passing within inches of the ground, then he flapped, catching the wind, going with it. Rising. Rising.

The snake became a cobra again, striking. He dodged and flew higher. The forest spread out beneath him like a carpet. He soared toward a distant mountain peak. The snake's strikes slowed. Erik made one last mighty flap of his wings, then let the cobra fall toward a rocky death below.

Elated, he soared and the breeze took him again until he once again became formless, riding the wind. His vision grew hazy. His world gray.

"Erik?"

He heard her voice. Near.

"Erik. You okay?"

A cool hand on his forehead.

"You're feverish."

He opened his eyes and saw Nicole. He reached toward her with a shaky hand. "I'm okay. My stomach." He tried to stand and fell back. "Bathroom. Quick." She helped him to the bathroom where he collapsed onto the toilet with more diarrhea, then he went to bed where he slept, dreaming vivid nonsensical dreams.

He regained consciousness in the predawn gray, weak and dehydrated, yet strangely rejuvenated, as if some new power animated him. Nicole slept soundly beside him.

After showering, he ate a hearty breakfast, then fixed a tray and brought it up to her. She opened her eyes when he sat on the edge of the bed.

"Morning, beautiful. How's my favorite baby sitter?"

She blinked at the tray. "Thank you. Don't you feel sick?"

"I'm feeling great." He fluffed a pillow and put it behind her, then set the tray on her lap.

"You sure acted strange." She took a sip of orange juice and attacked her French toast while Erik gave her the details of his experience.

"That explains a lot," she said when he finished. "You had me scared."

"What did I do?"

"First your eyes glazed over, then you started talking in that weird language."

"You have it on tape?"

She nodded. "You acted scared and started swinging your arms and kicking. I was afraid you might hurt one of us, but you settled down. Then you sang an eerie song or a chant. Your jaw quivered. You made some sounds that I think were more animal cries. After that you got real quiet, then the fever and diarrhea."

Erik couldn't stop himself from smiling. "I think I've seen part of my past, but better than that, I've learned something."

"What did you learn?"

"That I have a choice."

CHAPTER TWENTY SEVEN

Erik drove to the zoo and checked in with security, telling them he'd be working all night. After setting up a cot in his office, he took a stroll down to the tiger's pit to visit the Bengal he had taken to calling Tony. He found the big cat lounging majestically on a rock, high in the rear of the pit.

"Hey, partner. How's it going?"

The cat looked over and let out a low growl. Erik climbed the rocks and sat next to it, stroking it behind the ear as he spoke. "Listen, buddy. You and me, we have a special connection, you know? You're the first one -- I don't know, what should I call it?" Tony yawned and put his head on Erik's lap. Erik put his arms around the cat's neck. "You're the first one to talk to me." He felt the tiger's purr vibrating against him. "There's something I need to try. Will you help?"

Tony rolled over onto his back and put his paws in the air.

"Oh, I get it. I scratch your front, you scratch my back, right?"

Tony pawed at the air. Erik scratched the tiger's chest, then whispered what he wanted to try in the its ear before going back to his office where he stretched out on the cot. As he drifted off to sleep, he concentrated on Tony, waking up an hour later feeling as if he had only been asleep a minute. Without knowing why, he turned around on the cot and put his head where his feet had been, then thought of Tony again and fell asleep...

...opening his eyes in the darkness, recognizing his heightened smell and sharpened vision. Like the jaguar, only different. He saw the pit and the gate he had come through earlier. Putting his paws out in front, he stretched, then leaped down from his perch and paced back and forth across the front of the enclosure. He liked the tiger's body. It felt stronger, longer, and more agile.

He covered every inch of the pit, exploring it with his sight and smell, detecting things he had never sensed before. The overwhelming predatory urge he felt from the jag did not take possession of him, only a strong curiosity and a feeling of control.

After inspecting the pit, he found an obscure corner where he extended his claws and scratched in the dirt. When he felt satisfied, he hopped back up to his perch, lay down and went to sleep…

…jumping awake at the sound of his cell phone alarm. Reaching over, he shut it off, trying to assimilate his strange surroundings. When he realized where he was, he hustled down to the tiger pit. Tony lay dozing on his rock. Erik took a deep breath and let himself in through the rear gate. He wanted to run over to the corner of the enclosure, but decided to let Tony know he was there first so he wouldn't startle him. The cat greeted him with a rumbling purr. Erik patted him, then the two went to the corner of the pit.

"Yow!" he yelled raising his fist in the air. "Tony, look at that!" He pointed to the scratchings in the dirt.

The message read:

YOU'RE AN ANIMAL

CHAPTER TWENTY EIGHT

Nicole came to the door in a blue satin bathrobe, yawning, her hair ruffled. "What are you doing here so early?"

Erik took her into his arms, pulled her close and kissed her. "I've figured it out."

She wrapped her arms around him, then he picked her up and carried her to her bedroom where he dropped her on the bed.

"What did you figure out?"

He kicked off his shoes, unbuttoned his shirt and pants and jumped onto the bed, crawling on all fours.

She giggled. "What are you doing?"

He growled and undid the tie on her bathrobe with his teeth, letting her robe fall open.

"What's gotten into you?"

He climbed on top of her, kissing her neck and ears. She shuddered and moaned as he worked his way down toward her breasts.

"I'm an animal." He pulled off her panties with his teeth and wriggled out of his clothes.

After they made love, he told her what he had done with Tony. She listened, mouth open, blinking in astonishment. "You can go into any animal you want?"

He nodded. "I want to show you and Fritz. Will you help?"

"Sure." She studied him a moment, then hugged him. "You learned this from taking that horrible plant?"

"That horrible plant is part of my past. It's taught me that I have a choice about what animal I can go into. Do you know what this means?"

She shook her head. "You're getting ahead of me."

"My ability has been evolving out of my control. I've been doing it, but I haven't been fully conscious of it. I couldn't do anything in my dreams because I didn't realize I was really doing it. Now that I know what I can do, there won't be any more murders."

"It must have been horrible to live with."

He lowered his voice. "Now I'm in control. Master of the Animals. Maybe I can go to the jag and lead it into a trap."

Nicole didn't answer.

He recognized her worried look and drew her toward him. "Don't worry, babe," he whispered. "It's over. No more nightmares. I'll use my abilities to help Lieutenant Mitchell find the jag."

She squeezed him tighter.

Erik went to the zoo that night and slept on the cot, anxious to repeat his success with another animal. Before going to sleep he took a stroll through the compound looking for a subject. He decided on an elephant scheduled to be shipped out to the Franklin Park Zoo in Boston.

Lying on the cot, he closed his eyes, "feeling" his thoughts as he envisioned the elephant. Remembering his experience of the night before, he turned himself around on the cot, experimenting by putting his head at all four cardinal points. The image of the elephant in his mind felt sharpest on his third try. He went to sleep in that position and felt himself drifting…

…until the semi-darkness of the compound filled his senses. His metabolism felt slower and his vision dimmed, but his thoughts felt clear. The musky scents of the compound smelled stronger -- his nose -- a trunk! And his ears. Flopping down on the side of his head. He flapped them as his eyes adjusted, then played with his trunk, sniffing the ground and curling it before raising it above his head to trumpet his victory by letting out a high-pitched blast. The power of the sound thrilled him.

He lumbered over to the front of the cage, amazed at how slow and awkward he felt in comparison to the agile movements of a cat or the graceful flight of a bird. Welcoming the absence of any predatory drive or apprehension that came with being a quarry, he felt content to chew on the hay that had been left for him. It tasted surprisingly good.

He let his trunk fall to the ground and dragged it in the dirt keeping the message short and to the point. When he finished, he plodded back to the rear of the cage, let out a tiny trumpet blast to celebrate his success, then closed his eyes and faded into the darkness.

He opened his eyes and heard Fritz's clock in the next office cuckooing three times. Throwing on his pants and shoes, he went to the compound. Next to the bars at the front of the cage he saw the letters:

OK

rubbed into the dirt.

"Thank you very much, Mr. Elephant." Erik said, smiling.

He repeated the experiment twice more that night, once with a gray timber wolf and once with a gazelle. To insure success, he changed the position of his head until his thoughts of the animal he wanted to experience felt strongest.

He discovered that distance was not a factor, only the orientation of his head. All he had to do was hold the image of the animal in his mind, think of its location, and point his head in the right direction.

The next night he slept in his bed at the town house and went to three different animals in separate parts of the zoo, leaving a message to himself in each spot. Twice, he tried to go from one animal to the next, but he could only go from where he slept to the animal and back again. If he wished to inhabit another animal, he had to come back to his body and "pass through" as if the brain capacities of the animals were not powerful enough to project his thoughts.

He arose early on Monday, went to the zoo, and found his message in all three cages.

"Good morning," he said when Fritz came into the office. "How was your weekend?"

Fritz poured himself a cup of coffee. "My weekend was fine." He took a sip and nodded toward Erik. "You're in early this morning and I see that your mood has improved. You must have had a good time."

"You might say that." He smiled. "Tell me, can you work late tonight?"

"There is a problem?"

"I've made a little discovery. I want to share it with you."

Fritz's bushy eyebrows raised. "If I know you, my friend, there is no such thing as a little discovery. How long do I need to stay?"

"You can go home at your regular time and come back at nine. Nicole will meet you here."

"And what of you?"

"I'll show up a little later."

After making preparations at the zoo, Erik drove home. His excitement made it hard to fall asleep, but he finally lost consciousness, drifting until...

...he barely heard their voices.

"It's getting late," Fritz, said. "Are you sure nothing's happened?"

"I'm getting a little anxious myself, but I'm sure he'll be here."

He looked out from the cage he had hidden behind the office. His eyesight seemed close to normal but his body felt odd. Furry, almost human, and somehow out of proportion. He reached up with his paw, undid the latch on his cage and let himself out. Waddling toward the office door, he reached forward with his long forearms and propelled himself, first with his paws, then with his feet.

He crept in and found Nicole and Fritz sitting together by his desk. "A chimp!" she said, pointing to Erik.

"How did he get loose?" Fritz started toward him.

Erik tried to vocalize a response, but only chimp sounds came out. He backed away and ran to his desk where he found a pencil. He scribbled on his desk blotter in large wiggly letters.

I'M ERIK

Hoffelder strode toward the desk. "Come here, you!"

Erik chattered and pointed to the blotter with the pencil, then leaped out of Hoffelder's reach, scuttled around the older man and hopped up into Nicole's arms, hugging her.

"Here, give him to me," Hoffelder said.

He kissed Nicole on the cheek, chattered softly and pointed toward the desk. "He wants you to look on the desk."

Hoffelder turned and his head jerked back. "This can't be."

"What is it?" Nicole said.

"Must be a joke."

Erik leaped out of her arms and jumped up and down shaking his head.

Nicole stared, wide-eyed. "You did this?"

He nodded.

Fritz stood next to the desk, mouth open, bushy eyebrows arched in surprise. "This can't be."

Erik made a pushing motion with his paws.

"He wants you to back up," Nicole said.

"This is ridiculous. A chimp telling me what to do."

"Not just a chimp."

Hoffelder backed away and Erik scuttled up to the chair, turned his computer on and began hitting keys. His paws felt awkward, so he settled for the hunt and peck method of typing.

DON'T BE AN OLD HAUSFRAU, FRITZ!

"I don't believe it!"

He chattered and pecked at some more keys.

YOU BETTER BELIEVE IT OR I'LL MAKE A MONKEY OUT OF YOU.

Fritz grabbed the arm of a chair and lowered himself into it. "I'm too old for this." He pulled a handkerchief out of his pocket and wiped his brow.

Erik hopped out of the chair and went over to Nicole. When she leaned down he patted her on the cheek and kissed her, then went back to the computer.

I'M APE OVER YOU, BABE.

She burst into laughter. Erik climbed down from the chair, went over to Fritz and held out a paw. Fritz grasped it and shook his head. "If I weren't shaking your hand -- I mean paw, I wouldn't believe it."

Erik crossed the office and pushed another chair next to the computer. Taking Nicole by the hand, he led her to it. When she sat, he hopped back up on his chair and tapped on the keyboard.

MY BODY IS SLEEPING AT HOME. AFTER I LEAVE YOU CAN CALL ME THERE. I DON'T WANT ANYONE TO KNOW.

I DON'T WANT THE ATTENTION.   IT WILL BE OUR
SECRET.

He turned in his chair and looked Nicole in the eye and shook her
hand, then did the same with Fritz before turning back to the screen.

I WISH DAD COULD HAVE BEEN HERE TO SEE THIS.

No one spoke, then Erik started hitting the keys again.

NOW THAT I'M FULLY CONSCIOUS OF MY ABILITIES,
THERE IS NO LONGER A PROBLEM WITH THE JAGUAR IN
THE MOUNTAINS.

"That was you?" Fritz whispered.
Erik kept hitting the keys.

THAT PART OF MY ABILITY WAS OUT OF CONTROL. IF I
COULD, I'D TURN MYSELF IN, BUT NO ONE WOULD
BELIEVE ME. I HAVE TO LOCATE THE JAGUAR SO IT CAN
BE TRAPPED OR KILLED.

"Whatever I can do to help, let me know."
THANKS.
"As far as I'm concerned, we're in this together," Nicole said.
"All of us," Fritz added.
Erik took her hand, reached for Fritz and put all their hands
together, then he hopped out of the chair and ran back downstairs.
Fritz and Nicole followed him to the cage where he let himself in,
closed the door and snapped the lock.

CHAPTER TWENTY NINE

Six weeks passed without any sightings of the killer jaguar. Erik tried to find it by picturing it in his thoughts, but his dreams remained peaceful and under his command as he went from animal to animal, experiencing reality through each unique set of perceptions.

When no trace of the jag could be found, the National Park Service disbanded its search with the belief that the animal had died, been shot, or captured by a private party.

One day in late summer, Erik and Fritz performed surgery on an antelope that Erik had dreamed of the night before. While inside he felt pain in the animal's midsection. On his recommendation, Fritz operated and found that the animal had eaten a piece of wire that perforated its stomach and gave it peritonitis.

"You certainly made an accurate diagnosis." Fritz nodded toward the bloody piece of wire lying on a tray. "A little time on antibiotics and our friend will be fit as a fiddle." He tightened the last suture while Erik picked up the bloodied instruments. "What a research clinic wouldn't pay for your talents!"

"I'm happy the way things are. I plan to go into every animal in the zoo and give them a physical from the inside out."

Fritz nodded. "We'll have a healthy population and some good research. You don't have any problem moving from animal to animal?"

"I have to come back to my body first."

Fritz put antiseptic on the wound and dressed it. "I see. It seems that you -- what is that word? Project?"

"Yeah, project. Good word. Hadn't thought about it that way before."

"And what of your experiments with the plants?"

The image of the jaguar and snake flashed in his mind. "I don't want to do that anymore." He nodded toward the sedated antelope. "I'll learn enough from these animals. My experience with that vine jolted something in me. I still want to find out about my past, but the present is more important. The past is gone. Right now is alive, well, and living in the form of a dark-haired, head-turning beauty. Which would you pick?"

Fritz chuckled and pulled off his gloves. "A wise choice."

Erik lowered his voice. "All I want is to live my life with Nicole in a normal, uneventful manner. Sure, I have this connection with animals, but I like it the way it is. No one else needs to know. You're happy working with me the way things are, right?"

"If you became famous there wouldn't be a moment of peace."

"That's why I want to keep our working arrangement secret."

More than anything, Erik wanted things to stay peaceful, but his guilt about the Sierra killings ate at him like a parasite, gnawing its way into his conscience. He called Nicole before leaving the zoo, then stopped off at Fillipi's and picked up a pizza. By the time he got home, she had a bottle of Zinfandel opened, candles lit, and the table set.

"Nothing like a romantic pizza," he said setting the box on the table. He stole glances at her while they ate in silence, admiring the way the soft glow of candlelight played across her features.

"I have a little favor to ask," he said after they finished.

She took a sip of wine. "What is it?"

He picked up his wine. "Let's go into the den."

She smiled. "Sounds like a come on."

"Nothing like that."

"Oh?" She looked disappointed. "Okay." She led him into the den, directed him toward the recliner and stretched out on the couch. "What's on your mind?"

"The jaguar."

"Nightmares again?"

"It's just that -- well, I feel guilty."

She sat up. "You and I both know you had no control over it, but you're convinced you were part of it."

"I was." He sighed. "Watching those murders was horrible enough, but then lying about it, letting Lieutenant Mitchell think I was so smart and observant."

"Would it make you feel better if you told him?"

He nodded. "Even if I could, what would he do? Go and tell someone there's a zoologist who becomes a jaguar and kills people?"

"How would you tell him?"

"I could give him a demonstration. Would you help?"

"You don't even have to ask."

He dropped his head, struggling to keep the emotions that welled up inside of him in check. "All those people. Dead. I watched."

"You can't bring them back."

"If only I could've..."

"Only you know what happened, and you've admitted that you're not responsible. Quit blaming yourself. Face the guilt and realize that it's unfounded, then let it go."

"I couldn't stop it." His voice shook and his face grew hot. Tears blurred his eyes. "Dammit!" He wiped them off with the back of his sleeve. "I wanted to, but I couldn't," he whispered.

"I know," she said softly. She got up from the couch and came over to the recliner.

"I feel so stupid," he sobbed.

She sat on the arm of the recliner, hugged him, and stroked his hair. "Don't be ashamed of crying. Let it out. You've been holding it in for a long time. It needs to come out."

Her words released a torrent of sobs. Tears spilled down his face. "I couldn't stop it," he whispered.

CHAPTER THIRTY

E rik sat in his UCSD office the following morning, staring at the phone, knowing he had to call, not knowing what to say.

Hey, Scott, I haven't been up front about this. I let things get out of hand. I can go into an animal's mind while I'm sleeping. That's right, it was me in that jag. I knew you didn't think I was that smart. What the hell am I talking about? Well, I couldn't help myself...

He took a deep breath and punched Mitchell's number into his cell phone. After two rings a female voice came on the line.

"National Park Service. Lieutenant Mitchell's office. How may I help you?"

"Is the lieutenant in?"

"Sorry, he's out in the field."

Erik had a strong urge to hang up. "Umm, yes," he heard himself saying. "Could you have him call Erik Simpson?"

He gave her his number and hung up feeling hot and prickly. A bead of sweat slipped down the small of his back. He left the office, glad he had a morning lecture to occupy his mind.

When he came back that afternoon, he had all but forgotten about his call to Mitchell until his phone rang.

"I got a message you called," Mitchell said. "What's up?"

"I know the jag hasn't been a problem lately. This is probably going to sound weird, but -- well I thought I should tell you that I've..." I've been watching the murders of all those people, he thought. "I've uncovered some new information about the cat." The last sentence

129

tumbled out as though he were spitting out something bitter.

"You think it's still around?"

"I've discovered something you need to know."

"What is it?"

"It's complicated. Can't tell you over the phone."

A pause. "You feeling all right? You sound funny. Everything okay?"

"I'm fine. I can't explain it. It's something I have to show you. Can you make it down to San Diego?"

"It's that important?"

"I wouldn't ask if it weren't."

Mitchell sighed. "You came running when I called, so I owe you that. I'll be out in the field for the next couple of days. I'll probably have to stay overnight, but I can make it down on Thursday. Say around three."

"Dinner's on me."

"I'll call if I get hung up. Otherwise I'll meet you at the zoo. It'll be nice to meet under less sickening circumstances. The aftermath of a mauling is a hell of a time to make friends."

A series of ghastly images flashed through Erik's mind. Mitchell's features swam into view at the end of them. Sweat trickled down his armpits and a shiver passed through him. "Amen to that."

"I'll be there. This better be good."

Erik let out a nervous laugh. "Believe me, it'll be worth your while."

"How do you feel, now that you know he's coming?" Nicole asked. She and Erik sat together having a late lunch at a deli on campus. She wore a tan pleated skirt, a cream-colored blouse, and knee high patent leather boots.

"Part of me feels like I've signed my death warrant. Like it doesn't want to be found out, but I can't wait to get it out of the way."

"You'll feel better when it's over."

"It's driving me crazy. I wish it were over."

She reached across the table, rested her hand on his and squeezed.

He forced a smile, but her concerned look told him his act was wasted.

He couldn't sleep that night and couldn't focus on going inside an animal. Instead, his thoughts flashed like he had been plugged into a high-voltage power source. As the first gray streaks of daylight came into his room he slipped into an uneasy doze...

…and drifted aimlessly until a violent pull yanked him down with such force, he felt as if he'd been hit in the stomach. He opened his eyes and recognized the feeling. Duality and helplessness. The jag! He struggled against it and his perceptions grew hazy, then it pulled him down further, bringing his senses into sharp focus.

The High Sierras. Dawn. No sound but the wind soughing through the trees. His heightened smell told him of smaller prey. The quiet told him they sensed his presence, but he didn't care. A human was near. Only one. He sniffed the air again. He knew this one. Had been hunting it for weeks. Waiting for the right time.

He loped across a meadow and skirted its edge until he spotted a tent. Crouching, he crept forward, smelled his prey and listened. Though he couldn't see, he knew it intimately.

He inched closer. Watching. Waiting. One tent. One human. An easy kill. An easy escape.

Erik felt pinned and fascinated, as though an oppressive weight held him under water. He stopped struggling and for a moment the weight seemed heavier, then it lightened. He went down inside himself, letting his energy diminish, then in a burst of willpower, he tried to take full control of the jaguar and let out a roar. Something between a hiss and a growl escaped before the weight assaulted him again.

The tent moved. The cat sidled up alongside it and crouched beside its front. The sound of the zipper ripped through the morning stillness and a head poked out, followed by a gasp.

The shock of recognition numbed Erik.

The cat pounced, batting the head with a swipe of its paw. The head struck the ground with a sickening thud and the ranger slumped forward with a moan. Rolling over, his blue eyes looked up at the jaguar and blinked.

The cat straddled Mitchell, growled and opened its massive jaws. Mitchell's eyes widened.

Erik forced his eyes closed and threw himself into the darkness. The force held him. He shook himself, then felt something hard, (a fist?) striking his head. The distraction let him escape into the darkness…

His eyes snapped open. His breathing came ragged and his heart thumped against his ribs like a trapped animal. He put his hand to his chest and breathed deeply.

"Jesus Christ! Talk about nightmares."

He looked over at the clock. He had only been asleep for twenty minutes.

He tried to reassure himself, but his arguments weren't convincing. His mind rationalized, but his heart knew. The sinking feeling in his stomach told him the truth. He threw back the covers and fumbled for his address book and Mitchell's number. Though early, he tried it, but heard only a recording.

He called again at eight-thirty. When Mitchell's secretary came on the line, Erik's chest tightened.

"This is Erik Simpson, UCSD, San Diego Zoo. I need to talk to Lieutenant Mitchell. It's urgent."

"I'm sorry, he's out in the field. Won't be back 'til late this afternoon."

"I think he's in trouble."

"What makes you say that?"

"It's too complicated to explain."

"He's due for a radio check in the next half hour."

"Will you call me when he checks in?"

"Sure."

CHAPTER THIRTY ONE

Erik's heart felt as if it exploded when the phone rang. He snatched up his cell. "Hello," he said breathlessly.

"Hi, babe," Nicole said. "How you feeling this morning."

He sighed. "Edgy."

"Oh?"

"The jaguar."

Silence, then. "Want to talk about it?"

He heard Dr. Hoffelder coming into the office. "Maybe later."

"You sure you're okay?"

"I'll call you later." He ended the call and stared at his phone. An hour had passed since talking to Mitchell's secretary and still no call. After waking from his nightmare, Erik had gone straight to the zoo. He called Mitchell's office again.

"He hasn't checked in yet," the secretary said, "but there's no need for alarm. Sometimes the terrain blocks the signal. He'll radio when he finds a clear spot."

Two hours later he tried Mitchell's office again.

"He should've checked in by now," his secretary said. "We have two other men in the same sector. I've directed both of them to head toward the Lieutenant's area to make sure he's all right."

Later that night, Erik sat with Nicole at his kitchen table. "I'm afraid to go to sleep," he said.

"You look like hell. Did you get any sleep?"

He told her about his restlessness of the previous night and his lucid dream. "I keep telling myself it was only a dream, but..."

She put her hand on his cheek. "You need some sleep."

"I think it was real. What if I did do it and my ability is out of control?"

Nicole's eyes glazed as if looking past him, then came back into focus. "First off, you have no way of knowing if this last dream really happened or not. You said it's always different with this jaguar, right? Normally you have control, but with him, it's like something else is holding you down. Isn't that how you described it?"

"Yeah," he said tentatively.

"Something else is holding you down. Did you ever stop to think that maybe it *is* something else forcing you to take part? You haven't willed any of these actions, have you?"

He shook his head.

You kind of -- how did you put it? Went along as if it pulled you into it."

"You think something or someone else is doing this and I'm being forced to watch?"

"Let's put it this way. I know you and I know that you might go into an animal and be a predator, but only in the natural cycle of things. It's been instinctual on the animal's part. You did no more than follow what it does in its normal hunting and feeding cycle. There has never been any conscious will on your part to do any harm. You simply hunted as that animal."

"That's right."

"And I know you well enough to know that you would *never* consciously attack a human. It's not in your nature to act out such mindless violence."

Her words lightened his guilt. She was right. He hadn't consciously willed any of the attacks, in fact he had tried to stop them."

"Listen," she said. "Regardless of what happens, you need a good night's sleep." She rose from her chair, stood behind him and wrapped her arms around him. Her gentle touch and the scent of her perfume relaxed him. She kissed him on the neck, then massaged his shoulders. "I'm going to spend the night with you. I promise that if you have any dreams I'll wake you. Deal?"

He took her hand and kissed it. "Thanks."

She took him by the arm and led him to the bedroom. Five minutes after she tucked him in, he sank into a deep, dreamless slumber.

He woke at nine the next morning and called Mitchell's office again. "Hi, this is Erik Simpson, San Diego Zoo. Have they found the lieutenant yet?"

"No word from the field yet. We're getting a little worried. It's not like him to do this." Erik's stomach felt as though an icy hand had yanked it toward his feet. "We're sending out a search party."

"Where is he supposed to be?"

"Cedar Grove. Up in King's Canyon."

"Don't let those men go up there unless they're armed."

"You can't…"

"Who's in charge?"

"Captain Obeso."

"Put him on the line!"

"I'm sorry, but I can't…"

"Put him on the line!"

A moment later a man's voice came on the line. "This is Captain Obeso. What's the problem?"

"This is Erik Simpson, San Diego Zoo. I worked with Lieutenant Mitchell on the jaguar fatalities earlier this year."

"I remember. Scott spoke very highly of you. What can I do for you, Mr. Simpson?"

"There's no time to explain, but I've uncovered evidence that leads me to believe the jaguar is still loose. Don't send anyone up there unarmed. I need to help you in the search. Can you send me a chopper?"

"You feel that strong about it?"

"I'll stake my reputation on it."

"We'll have one down to you in a couple of hours. Lindbergh Field?"

"That's right."

"We'll rendezvous at the Cedar Grove ranger station."

"See you there."

Captain Obeso was a spindly, balding man with heavy-lidded eyes and a drooping mustache. He reminded Erik of a bear just awakened from hibernation. His pot-belly added to the caricature.

"Mitchell was dispatched up into this area," Obeso said, pointing to a large relief map of Kings Canyon, letting the pointer come to rest on Lookout Peak. "To investigate some reports of increased bear activity, but we may be up against something else."

A low murmur passed through the room. Erik felt twelve sets of eyes on him.

"As you all know, we had problems earlier this year up in Big Pine and down in Bearpaw Meadow with an escaped jaguar. He attacked twice but hasn't been seen or heard from in months." He gestured toward Erik. "We're lucky to have Erik Simpson from the San Diego Zoo to help us. He's the man responsible for identifying the attacker as a jaguar in the last two incidents. He has reason to believe we may be dealing with the same animal. I want you men to listen to what he says, and I want you to follow his orders as if they were coming from me. Any questions?"

The room filled with voices again, but no one asked a question. Obeso held up a hand to quiet them. "Okay, Erik, the floor's yours."

Erik stood and nodded toward the rangers. "If we are up against the jag, there's no room for error. He's not your average Sierra resident and he's more than cunning. His behavior is totally unpredictable. He can outsmell, outrun, and outsmart you. Make no bones about it, gentlemen. This is a dangerous animal. A deadly hunter."

One of the rangers toward the back of the room raised his hand. Erik acknowledged him.

"What makes you think he's up here now?"

The question caught Erik off guard. "As I told you, his behavior is unpredictable. I've been doing some studies based on what I do know. The evidence I found at the other sites and the maps I've been studying, have given me an area that he would have staked out as his own." Okay, if they'll buy that I'll give 'em one more good lie, he thought. "Though we haven't seen or heard from him in months, I made some predictions. I pray that I'm wrong, but when I heard Lieutenant Mitchell was missing…"

His throat closed. He took a deep breath and continued. "We have limited manpower. It's imperative that we stay in pairs and in close radio contact. Everyone should be armed with a partner in sight. No more than twenty-five feet away."

"Do we really need to stay that close?" someone asked.

"He's made five kills so far. We can't take any chances."

Erik teamed up with Obeso and the other rangers paired off, making a systematic search of the area.

"Is there a meadow near here?" Erik asked, as the images from his dream passed through his mind making his stomach queasy.

"A few of them. Why do you ask?"

"The jag would probably have been prowling around a meadow. Was there one up where Mitchell would have camped?"

Obeso pulled out a map and scrutinized it a moment, then jabbed with his finger. "Right here."

"That's where we'd better start."

Erik's breath caught when he recognized the meadow from the top of a rise forty five minutes later. "My God," he whispered.

Obeso looked at him and frowned, but didn't say anything. Erik broke into a run until he reached the edge of the clearing where he stumbled and fell. He saw the grass pressed down.

Obeso caught up with him. "You all right?"

Erik scrambled to his feet without answering and bolted across the open space following the path he had taken in the dream. He felt dizzy and his world took on a dreamlike quality. His legs pumped, straining, each step feeling endless. His chest ached.

He saw the top of the tent over the high grasses and his legs went slack. He lunged forward. The back of the tent swam into view. Part of him wanted to stop, but the other part had to know. He ran the last few steps, sliding as he rounded the front of the tent.

The flap hung open. No sign of life. He studied the area in front of the tent until his breath snagged in his throat, feeling like a claw embedding itself in his neck. *Paw prints*.

Hot tears filled his eyes. Obeso came up behind him. "What the hell?"

Erik pointed to the ground with a trembling hand. Marks in the dirt where something had been dragged. He followed them, Obeso behind him, neither man speaking.

They led to a cluster of rocks. He saw a pair of boots sticking out from the side of a boulder. "Oh, God, no. Not again!" His voice shook. The sun grew dimmer as if a dark cloud passed in front of it. He stepped closer and saw a hand. Something scratched into the dirt beside it:

SUÁNA-KAHÍ-MÁ

Erik recognized the words. No way Mitchell would know…

He took the final step.

Mitchell lay propped against the rock, his shirt drenched black, his head nearly severed, tilted up to the sky at an impossible angle, his blue eyes wide, reflecting the emptiness. A thick swarm of flies covered him.

"Oh my God," Obeso uttered as darkness closed in. Erik's legs gave way. He heard Obeso vomiting as everything went gray. The scratching on the ground flitted through his mind as his last conscious image.

Suána-kahí-má. Kahi of the red jaguar. The third strongest Kahi, known for producing visions in red.

CHAPTER THIRTY TWO

Buzzing.

In his head. No. Outside him. A gentle breeze blew carrying with it a pungent smell. He gagged and opened his eyes. The buzzing came from flies, the smell from the same place. He turned away and saw the pasty face of Captain Obeso.

"You all right, Simpson?" he whispered hoarsely.

Erik's stomach spasmed and his body felt hot and prickly. His sweat felt cold. He didn't feel strong enough to speak, so he nodded. Obeso crawled away and heaved again, then barked orders into his radio. Erik glanced back at Mitchell's fly-infested body, then dragged himself away from the corpse and propped himself up against a tree.

Obeso joined him a few minutes later. "How did you know?"

"I saw signs by the meadow." His own voice sounded weak and strained, but his shock quickly gave way to anger. "I'll get that son-of-a-bitch if it's the last thing I do," he growled.

Obeso wiped his mouth on his sleeve. "Help's on the way. We'll get the fucker."

Erik nodded.

"Jesus, what a brute," Obeso said, shaking his head. "Why didn't it eat its kill?"

Because I wasn't there, Erik thought. "I told you he's behaving unusually." Son-of-a-bitch purposely left Mitchell there for us to find. Throwing it in our face.

"What about that message Mitchell left?" Obeso said, breaking in on his thoughts. "I think it's Spanish. Make any sense to you?"

Erik shook his head. Suána-kahí-má. Looks like Mitchell wrote it, but there's no way in the world he would know. No way anyone would know, unless... He struggled to his feet, fought back a wave of dizziness and forced himself to go back to the corpse. The message *had* been scratched in the dirt by the jag. Someone or something could do the same thing he could.

Vivid images flickered through his mind. The jaguar hunting him as a boy. His nightmares. The feeling of being separate, yet part of it. The helplessness. He was innocent. Not a murderer. The release he felt gave him a brief moment of elation until he looked down at the lifeless body and the glazed, fly-infested eyes that stared at nothing. A black mass of flies burrowed into the exposed tissue of Mitchell's severed neck.

His whole body felt chilled.

Hot tears came with wracking sobs. He waved the flies away from Mitchell's unseeing gaze, put his hand on the cold, stiff flesh of his eyelids and forced the dead man's eyes closed.

"Don't worry partner," he whispered. "I'll get him -- for you *and* Dad."

Less than three hours later, shotgun toting rangers and federal agents with .45's on their hips milled about, waiting for Erik's word as he showed Captain Obeso and agent Schmitten the direction the jaguar had taken. Anger was the only thing that kept him lucid.

He set off following the jaguar tracks, pointing them out to Schmitten so his men could take casts.

"As soon as you give the word, we'll be after him," Schmitten said, his voice low and full of conviction. "Son-of-a-bitch isn't going to get away with this. Piece of shit got one of ours. *One of ours!* He fucked with the wrong people this time. National Guard'll be here in a couple of hours. They're bringing in their best K-9 tracking teams, but it's getting late. I don't want any men combing the woods in the dark. If it's all right with you, we'll brief them this afternoon and deploy at daybreak."

Erik nodded, his gaze meeting Schmitten's angry glare. He sensed the hurt behind the anger. Mitchell had been a friend of Schmitten's too.

"I want you to brief them," Schmitten said. "We don't want to lose anyone else. Give them everything you know about its habits, what to watch out for -- and we're not taking any chances. Orders are shoot to kill."

"Amen to that," Obeso said.

"I have a good idea of where he's headed," Erik said.

Schmitten smacked his palm with his fist. "You point us in the right direction. Leave the hunting to us. We'll find the motherfucker."

Erik's chest tightened and the words flew from his mouth before he could stop them. "I'm not leaving the hunting to anybody. I appreciate the help, but I'm going to find him. This is – is…" his voice dropped. "Personal."

Schmitten shook his head. "Sorry, but we can't have…"

"Bullshit!" Grief and anger exploded in one exquisite combination. "You can't take this away from me. I've been on this from the beginning!" Bastard's been haunting me long enough, he thought. Time to end it once and for all. Uh-uh, buddy, you aren't getting in my way. This is between me and the jag.

Schmitten studied Erik with smoldering eyes, but didn't say anything more.

"We need him," Obeso cut in. "You've seen what he can do. He knows animals. Hell, he's probably safer than any of us."

The fire went out in Schmitten's eyes. He shook his head. "You're right."

Erik looked at Obeso, who winked.

"It may take awhile," Erik said. "He moves fast."

"It doesn't matter how long it takes," Schmitten said. "We're not giving up until I see him dead."

Three hours later, Erik felt as if he were lecturing a class at UCSD, only this group had guns; uniformed rangers, National Guardsmen and plainclothes FBI. He described how a jaguar hunted and how its keen sense of smell and hearing would alert it to the presence of so many humans, making it difficult to apprehend.

"We'll be going out at daybreak." He scanned the faces of the crowd. "Stay in groups of three…" He recognized one of the rangers. From where? The man stared at him. Dark hair. Dark skin. Dark eyes. Defiant. Like the animals -- the coyote, the chimp, the snake, the Indian he had seen in the picture. He remembered the vision he had under the influence of Ayahuasca. The ceremony.

"You said it usually stalks its prey at dawn or dusk?" someone asked from the back of the group.

"Huh? Oh, yes. That's the behavior of a normal jaguar. Keep that in mind, but remember, this one's behaving out of character, so use extreme caution."

He looked back to the dark ranger, but the man had disappeared. Erik stifled the urge to run into the crowd and find him.

"If there are no more questions..."

There were.

After answering them, Erik stepped into the crowd to search for the man whose gaze had unnerved him, but he found no sign of him. He kicked at the ground in frustration, then sat down against a tree to think. It had to be his imagination. Too much stress – then again, the scratchings in the dirt next to Scott weren't.

The hunt would start at dawn. Hundreds of human beings filling the forest with their scents and sounds. Their false sense of stealth would sound like the roar of an F-16 to the sensitive ears of a jaguar, their scents like a garbage truck on a hot day. Hunting him in this manner was close to futile. There was a better way to hunt him, without the telltale signs of humans. Erik would embark on that hunt tonight, before this human mass of fear, sweat, and nervous banter disrupted the woods with their presence.

CHAPTER THIRTY THREE

Erik lay awake that night in a sleeping bag that the National Guard had loaned him, thinking about what the jaguar had done to Mitchell. The jaguar, the defiant stares, the animals he had confronted, the chimp and the attacking snake -- now the dark-haired man he had seen yesterday. Something about him.

He knew that whatever killed Mitchell was also responsible for the death of his father. So many things puzzled him, but one thing he knew for sure. Only he could stop the killing.

His thoughts gravitated toward the High Sierra animals. Which one was a good hunter? Better still, he needed a tracker with a keen sense of smell. He would be up against a master hunter. Which animal?

Pressing his palms to his eyes, he went through a mental list of the animals he knew until one jumped out at him. Ursus Americanus. The Black Bear. With a sense of smell 500 times stronger than a human's, it could easily catch the scent of something foreign. Remembering his experience with the Sun Bear at the Zoo, Erik pointed his head in the proper direction.

He thought he might have a problem getting to sleep, but the events of the day and the outpouring of emotion he experienced had exhausted him. Sleep came easily.

Soon after drifting into unconsciousness, the "breeze" came and carried him along until he floated downward and his awareness shifted.

He sensed darkness and found himself in a cave. He stood and stretched his bulky frame, then climbed up out of its opening. Working his way up to a high spot, he raised his snout in the air and sniffed.

Myriad smells mingled like colors in a painting. He separated each one in his mind, discarding those he knew to be familiar, focusing on the two that felt out of place. The unmistakable scent of humans and the unfamiliar, dangerous scent of the intruder, cutting across everything else like a bold stroke of red in an otherwise gentle pastel.

He tracked both scents to the spot where they met. Here the human smells felt overpowering, but the darker smell lingered. He skirted the edge of the meadow, stopping every few feet to sniff the air. At the far end of the field, the intruder's scent split off on its own course. Erik followed, leaving the human smells behind.

The scent of the jaguar grew stronger.

He climbed rocks, followed streambeds and crossed open spaces, his confidence growing with the freshness of the trail. The alien scent grew stronger. Stepping up his pace, he loped through the night until the smell filled his whole being, teasing the rage that grew inside him. The trail proved to be easy to follow.

It cut to the right, then led down an incline into a canyon. The scent here struck him as the strongest he'd encountered all night. Erik followed the canyon to the end, finding a wall too steep to climb. Bewildered, he turned and realized the canyon had three sides and one exit. Where could the jag have gone?

As if in answer to his question he heard a hiss. The massive heart pumping inside him jumped, filling him with adrenaline. He looked up to an overhanging ledge.

Two glowing yellow orbs held him, their defiant glare unmistakable. Raising up on his haunches, he felt the hairs on his back bristle. The jaguar lunged before he reached full height. Falling backward, he felt its claws raking his throat. Its jaws found his shoulder. A roar of agony burst from him. He batted the jaguar aside and raised himself up again.

It leaped twice, then struck from behind, claws cutting into his hide, teeth sinking deep. If not for the breadth of his neck it would have snapped. He let himself fall backward, bringing his weight down on the jaguar. It hissed, wiggled out from under him and circled around in front, its demonic yellow eyes intent.

Erik swiped with his paw and jumped sideways. He had the strength, but he couldn't defeat it in this form. The cat had too much speed and agility. Erik wanted to leave the bear's body, but felt guilty for putting it in danger. He had no choice, but to fight.

The cat circled and leaped from the side. He saw a bright flash, then excruciating pain as a claw found its way to one of his eyes, blinding it. Spinning, he raked the cat's ribs with his own claws. It bounded away, hissing.

The fire in his eye distracted him and the jaguar hit again from his blind side, its teeth finding his throat. He wrapped his paws around it and pressed it to his chest. The two rolled to the ground locked to each other. He felt the cat's jaws sink into his throat as his paws clutched it. Darkness closed in, but he refused to let go.

Something snapped in his throat and warmth spilled down his chest. His breathing came in ragged spurts, each inhalation burning worse than the last, each exhalation growing more bubbly. Softer. He sensed approaching death and willed himself out of the bear, but with each dying gasp, his will grew weaker.

Grayness enveloped him.

He heard the cry of an eagle from somewhere above. His senses brightened as if a flashbulb had gone off, followed by darkness. With it came relief from his agony. He floated upward, still conscious, beneath him the jaguar backed away from the still form of the bear. Its life had ended.

Had his?

CHAPTER THIRTY FOUR

The eagle cried again, startling him. He heard the fluttering of wings, looked up and saw its silhouette swoop down and snatch him, carrying him off. The rhythm of its wings had a soothing effect, calming the pulse of his heart until the two beats became one.

He studied the intelligence and compassion behind the bird's eyes as it drew him up into the clear night sky. He felt like a child held close in the comfort of its mother's bosom. A burst of emotion propelled the word from him. "Dad?"

Once more, the bird spoke without sound, its voice filling his mind. *You are safe my son, but the danger is closing in. You have reached your thirtieth season. You must regain the lost knowledge of the Natema and restore the balance. Take back what is rightfully yours. You possess the amulet. It is you who must lead.*

"What do I have to do?"

You are the rightful Master of the Animals. You must seek out the Kai-ya-ree ritual and bring the light into your soul so you may drive out the Ooname and overcome the Suána-kahí-má.

"The Kai-ya-ree ritual. How will I know it?"

The Holy Flower of the North Star, The Cactus of the Four Winds, The Vision Vine, and The Flying Death. In these lie the key to your awakening.

He looked into the swirling colors of the eagle's eye. "But how will I know what to do?"

Remember.

"I can't…"

The eagle's eye brightened. Erik felt pressure on his head as if a spectral hand had grasped it, followed by a pleasant tingling and a popping sound. His thoughts went blank before a series of images flooded his mind like air rushing into a vacuum.

He smelled the jungle, heard drums, saw women scattering to the forest, dancing, chants, ceremonial feathers, saw himself. The ritual. The amulet.

The sound of the flapping wings dimmed. Erik's memories faded. No longer aware of the eagle's presence, he felt only the sensation of being carried along by the wind, then of floating downward...

...waking to the first blue streaks of approaching day shimmering behind a mountain peak. The smell of coffee filled the air. Erik climbed out of his sleeping bag and dressed, then sought out Obeso and Schmitten, finding them sitting next to a campfire sipping coffee. Obeso poured a cup and handed it to him.

"What's the plan of attack?" Schmitten said.

Erik played back his experience of the night before and remembered the canyon. "I have a good sense of where he's headed. Maybe even a general idea of where his lair is. It doesn't mean we'll find him, but it could narrow down the area we have to cover."

Obeso glanced at his watch. "We'll be ready to move out in forty-five minutes."

An hour later, Erik led them through the meadow, following the direction he had taken as the bear. The morning sun rose higher in the sky and beat down on them. They climbed the same rocks Erik had, followed streambeds and crossed open spaces. By late afternoon Schmitten wanted to stop.

"Just a little further," Erik said. "I think we're close to something."

"What makes you so sure?"

"I don't know. Instinct, I guess."

"If I hadn't seen you work last time, I wouldn't believe you, but I know what you can do. We'll give it another half hour."

Erik stepped up the pace, anxious to find the bear before nightfall. Twenty minutes later, he tensed, recognizing the canyon. "Pass the word down the line," he said under his breath. "I think we're near his lair." He wanted to run, but restrained himself. He didn't want any questions.

They topped a ridge and went down into the canyon. Erik smelled it before he spotted the bear's corpse. "There!" He pointed. "Looks like our friend left a calling card."

They trotted down to the remains of the bear. The jaguar had eaten some of this kill. What he had left, the smaller animals had begun devouring.

"It was him, all right," Erik said feeling guilty. "I can tell by the wounds. Besides, nothing else up here could do this to a bear."

"We may as well camp here for the night," Schmitten said turning away from the half-eaten carcass in disgust.

"There's no need for this poor bastard to be lying around stinking up the place," Obeso said. "If you've no objections, Erik, I'll have some men come down and bury it."

Erik nodded. "I've seen all I need to see."

"We'll put some men out on perimeter to guard the camp," Schmitten added.

"I doubt the jag's going to bother us with this many men," Erik said, "but it's a good idea just the same. Listen," he said, lowering his voice. "I need to go back to San Diego for a day or two to do some research. I might be on to something."

Schmitten frowned. "After all that shit you gave me about being in on this from the start? Now you're going to leave? Come on, man. You followed that cat for miles. We never would have come this far without you. You can't just leave."

"If I didn't think it important, I wouldn't, but I have to run down this lead."

"What is it?"

"I'll let you know when I find it."

Schmitten's angry glare bore into him for a moment before the man turned his back. "Great!" he muttered, then stormed away.

Obeso patted Erik on the back. "Don't worry about him. He'll cool off. I'll send a few men down with you. When you've found out what you want, get your ass back up here a.s.a.p.. We need you."

CHAPTER THIRTY FIVE

Erik found Dr. Gilbert in the corner of his lab hunched over a microscope. He waited until Gilbert stopped to jot a note before interrupting. "Excuse me, Dr. Gilbert."

The old man looked over his shoulder. "Erik! How are you?" He hopped off his stool and took Erik's hand. "I've been thinking about you. Since we last talked you've stirred my curiosity. I've been doing some of my own research."

"What did you find?"

"I may have discovered a connection to your past." He patted the stool next to his. "I don't know why I hadn't thought of it before, but when you came to me asking about the Vision Vine, I did some serious digging. I haven't been able to substantiate it, but twenty five or thirty years ago a Swedish botanist, his wife and child were lost in a fire in South America. They died close to where we found you. Phineas spent years researching this."

"He never said anything to me about it."

"Because he never knew the truth. The Swedish government lost the death certificates. I may have found them along with another telling piece of information."

Erik's heartbeat quickened. "What?"

"They never recovered the child's body."

"You think?" Erik's mind went blank. He opened his mouth but no words came. Gilbert studied him expectantly.

"The time frames match. I'm still working on it. If I get my hands on the rest of the papers, I'll contact you immediately."

"I appreciate it."

"No problem. Now tell me, how'd your study go with the Ayahuasca?"

"Thanks for the samples, and I appreciate all the books you lent me. They helped more than you can imagine."

Gilbert rested a beefy hand on Erik's shoulder. "I know you didn't take that vine and look at it under a microscope. What was it like for you? Did you see snakes and jaguars?"

Erik told him about his experience, giving most of the details he had gleaned from his past. As he spoke, Gilbert nodded as if recalling his own experience, his eyes widening behind his glasses at the high points, reminding Erik of an owl.

"Interesting," he said when Erik finished. "The similarities in experiences are remarkable."

Erik studied the older man. "How did you know I was going to take it?"

Gilbert chuckled. "Not many young men come to me asking about one of the most potent entheogenic plants in existence with the intent of studying its leaf structure."

"Why didn't you say something?"

"I didn't want to encourage you and I didn't want to discourage you either. You're a bright young man. With your background and what I know of it, your interest in Yajé didn't surprise me. You had a legitimate right to try it."

Erik shook his head and found himself smiling. "You old dog."

Gilbert burst into a hearty laugh until his face turned bright red. "I was right, wasn't I?"

"You were."

"I need your help," Erik blurted.

Gilbert's eyes narrowed behind his glasses. Their thick lenses exaggerated the effect. "What's on your mind?"

"I've learned something about my past from the visions I've had. I can't give you the specifics now, but I promise I'll tell you everything when it's over."

"All right, son. Tell me what it is you need."

"I need more plants and all the texts you can find."

Gilbert frowned. "Don't tell me. You want more Ayahuasca, a piece of the San Pedro cactus, and Datura."

Erik nodded. "And curare."

The owl eyes again. "Curare? Do you know how potent these plants are by themselves? Taken individually they can be lethal. Are you trying to kill yourself?"

"I know how crazy it sounds, but in one of my visions I remembered a ritual I participated in before the jaguar came after me. I want to duplicate it."

"How do you know it wasn't a hallucination?"

"I can't explain it, but I know."

Gilbert fell silent and his eyes took on a faraway look. Erik respected the silence until the older man's eyes came back into focus. "My heart tells me to let you do this, but my mind says no. If something happened I'd never forgive myself."

"I hate putting you in this position, but I have to rediscover my past. You may find some things for me in your research, you may not. I can't tell you how much I appreciate you taking the time to look and I don't want you to stop, but I have to discover things in my own way." He looked hard into Gilbert's eyes. "Think of it as an experiment. If I'm successful, I can give you a whole new perspective on the field -- an insider's view."

"And if you're not successful, you'll give me a guilty conscience. I couldn't live with the idea of helping you ruin yourself."

Erik stared down at the floor trying to decide how to persuade the man. He had to do the ritual. "If I don't get help from you, I'll go somewhere else, but I know you and trust your judgment. You have the knowledge and background I need. If you don't help me I'll go to Colombia if I have to. You can't stop me. All you can do is slow me down. Please, doc, trust me on this. As crazy as it sounds, I know what I'm doing. When I finish what I have to do, I'll come and tell you everything."

Gilbert stared out the window and paced back and forth for a long time before stopping at his bookcase and selecting a few volumes. "My better judgment tells me I'm making a mistake, but I believe you when you say you're going to do it anyway. All I can do is see that you go into this with both eyes open."

He walked over and put the books on the desk, then went to a cabinet on the far wall and selected samples. When he had them all, he locked the door to his lab, sat down with Erik, and explained the specifics of each plant, backing up his statements with passages from the text.

Erik left two hours later with four plant samples.

After stopping off at the townhouse for a shower and change of clothes, he grabbed his camping gear and some artifacts from his father's closet. Before leaving, he checked in with Nicole.

"Hello?" She said picking up on the first ring.

"It's Erik."

"Where have you been? I've been worried sick. Why didn't you call? What happened up in the mountains?"

"Mitchell didn't make it."

Silence came from the other end of the line.

"I'm the one who found him," Erik said, breaking it. "They called in the National Guard. We've been combing the woods looking for the jag."

"You're still up there?"

He didn't want to tell her he was home, but he couldn't bring himself to lie and he didn't have time to explain. As much as he wanted her with him, the legend said that if a woman witnessed the ritual it meant death. It didn't seem possible but nothing else that had happened to him seemed possible, either.

"I'm home, but I'm leaving. Could you call Fritz for me?"

"You don't want to see me?"

He heard the hurt in her voice. "I want to see you more than ever," he said. "But there's something I have to do."

"You're going to do something with those plants, aren't you?"

He didn't know what to say.

"Dammit, Erik, I should be there. Don't set foot outside that house until I get there. Do you hear me? Someone has to watch out for you."

"No matter what you think," he said. "I love you. Don't ever forget it." He hung up before she could respond. The phone rang as he gathered up his things and was still ringing when he went out the door.

CHAPTER THIRTY SIX

Erik drove north on I-15 in search of the right place to perform the ritual. It had to be a place of power. Turning off on route 74, he drove through Hemet, thinking that the mountains near Idyllwild would have a suitable place of power. He remembered an ancient Indian legend surrounding Tahquitz peak. The similarities to his own situation had ominous parallels.

The Indian chief Tahquitz had ruled over the valley until beautiful Indian maidens began disappearing. Tahquitz had been the one responsible for their murders. The other Indians sentenced him to death by fire, but his form disappeared as a spark flew out of the flames and drifted into the mountains where his evil spirit took abode in a cave closed by a huge stone. When the earth shook on the mountain, it meant that Tahquitz was trying to get out.

The son of Chief Algoot challenged him, only to be killed by the demon who had the ability to change form, then the chief himself challenged Tahquitz who took on the form of a serpent. A monumental battle followed and the serpent was thrown on a funeral pyre, but green wood had been used. Again his spirit escaped. He supposedly still haunted the region today, heralding his presence by the rumbling mountains.

The place where Tahquitz changed form and became a serpent was a place of power fitting for the ritual, Erik thought.

After obtaining a wilderness permit he hiked up from the trail head at Humber Park. Being midweek, he saw only birds, chipmunks, and squirrels on the trail.

Clouds packed the sky and the woods felt misty and damp, the air full of an earthy smell. No wind. The forest held an eerie stillness as though every living thing in it watched his approach. When the trail split at Saddle Junction he took the path up to Tahquitz Peak. As he neared it, the mist thickened and the wind grew stronger.

Veering off the trail, he hiked a mile or so until he stood near the base of the peak, then zig-zagged up its side until he found a small craterlike hollow halfway to the top, protected on all sides from the wind. He took off his pack and leaned it against a rock, then closed his eyes and calmed himself, rehearsing the ritual in his mind, examining each detail until he felt sure he had it all committed to memory.

After setting up four camp stoves, he took the four-ribbed pieces of San Pedro cactus, sliced them like bread and put them in a pan of water that he heated on the first stove. Next he took the Datura root, pounded it into a pulp and put it in another pot of boiling water, followed by mashed lengths of the vision vine, which he placed in a third pot. He did the same with a smaller portion of curare.

The better part of the day passed as he let the mixtures boil down to thick consistencies. Clouds pressed in at dusk, blanketing the mountainside. Thunder rumbled, shaking the mountain as if the spirit of Tahquitz beckoned him from the other side where he would soon be traveling in the world of serpents and jaguars. Shaking off a chill, Erik wrapped his coat tighter around him. The words of the eagle filled his mind, giving him strength.

You must assert yourself and regain the lost knowledge of Natema. Restore the balance and take back what is rightfully yours. You are The Master of the Animals. You must seek out the Kai-ya-ree ritual and bring the light into your soul so you may drive out the Ooname and overcome the Suána-kahí-má.

He took the first pot of the thickened essence of San Pedro and held it above his head, dancing and chanting, stopping only to bow toward the four cardinal points and to ask the spirit of the Cactus of the Four Winds to feed his inner power and guard him against the dark spirits of the underworld while guiding him toward the visions of his past. After a complete circuit, he stopped and downed the contents of the pot in one gulp, wincing at its pungent taste.

He picked up the second pot of Datura which had boiled down to a thick paste. Sitting on the ground, Erik bowed toward the north, touching his head to the ground, then he rubbed a dab of paste into his forehead, stripped off his shirt and massaged the rest into his abdomen.

As he finished, the initial effects of the cactus energized him. A slight dizziness passed through him, followed by a clearing of his faculties. A light numbness filled his body, then a sense of tranquility and detachment, as if his thoughts drifted toward another dimension.

Taking the tiny portion of curare, he mixed it with the brackish liquid he had extracted from the vision vine and downed it, gagging on its bitterness. He performed another short dance from memory, and felt his mind shifting, as if floating further from his body.

His heart beat faster. In spite of the cool temperature he sweated profusely. Unrolling his sleeping bag, he took off his clothes and climbed inside. By the time he lay down, he could hardly move. At least now, if he lost consciousness, his body would be protected from the elements; at least the physical ones.

He felt the urge to vomit and panicked, fearing he would choke, but paralysis rendered him helpless. His mind remained alert, but his body stayed rigid, refusing to obey his thoughts, trapping him in a prison of flesh. He forced himself to stay calm and the nausea passed.

The wind kicked up and thunder shook the mountain. The sky above and the rocks surrounding him flared as though multicolored lasers and strobe lights had turned on. He heard a hissing sound -- a jaguar? Snake? -- behind him, but he couldn't turn his head to look. The ground shook again and he felt a hot wind on his head as if something breathed on him.

The rocks around him began to melt, their substance dribbling to the ground like streams of different colored candle wax that took on the form of snakes, slithering toward him. He wanted to run, but his body remained inert.

The heat on his scalp increased and his vision darkened as a massive black jaguar's head blocked his view. Out of the corner of his eye he saw the snakes getting closer. The jaguar opened its jaws, its fetid breath suffocating him.

I'm dying.

Sparks flew through the air and his body rose, as though lifted by the wind. Thunder. The mountain rattled. The wind grew stronger and he rose faster, disappearing into the black maw of the jaguar. Stars raced toward him in a dizzying swirl as he spun still faster, hurtling through the air like a demented comet...

CHAPTER THIRTY SEVEN

His perceptions blurred, then snapped into focus. He was a child again, sitting in the corner of a grass house looking at picture books. Up on a wall he saw the plants Mommy had collected with the help of the dark-haired people.

He remembered coming here on a boat. Living in this place with the trees, the animals, and the dark-haired people with the funny colors on their faces who wore feathers. Where was Mommy? His chest tightened at the realization of her absence. "Mommee!" His body shook and then he sobbed. Tears spilled down his face. "Mommee!"

His cries stopped when he saw her. Joy welled in his heart. Her big blue eyes told him she loved him. She had her pretty yellow hair tied with a scarf that matched her eyes.

"What's the matter, baby? Did you get scared?"

He raised his hands and she scooped him up. Her touch thrilled him, then she hugged him and he lost himself in the comfort of her flowery smelling hair and soft skin. He hugged her and kissed her on the cheek as she stroked his hair, then he buried his face in the warmth of her bosom.

"Is he okay, Gretchen?"

He looked over Mommy's shoulder and saw Daddy, whose blue eyes smiled at him. His hair had the same color as Mommy's, only shorter.

"A little scare, that's all." She hugged him tighter and carried him into the other room. "It's almost bed time anyway. Would you like to give him a good night hug, Bjorn?"

"Sure."

She handed him to Daddy who gave him a solid hug. The whiskers on Daddy's face felt rough. Erik smelled traces of soap and sweat. Man smells. Daddy sat him on his knee and smiled. "How's my boy tonight? Ready to go to dream land?"

Erik shook his head. Daddy tickled him until he squealed and shook with giggles. Mommy took him back. "I'll not have you getting him excited at bedtime, Bjorn Skorksen," she chided, carrying him toward the bedroom. Erik peered over Mommy's shoulder at Daddy who smiled and winked, then he lost himself in Mommy's sweet smells and softness.

He cried when she set him on the bed because he didn't want her to go, so she stayed with him, lying beside him, singing softly until he fell asleep.

Hot orange woke him. He coughed and opened his eyes.

They burned. "Mommy! Daddy!" He cried and coughed again. It burned his throat. Thick smoke billowed into his room. He stood up on his bed and tried to run to Mommy and Daddy but the fire was too hot. The smoke too black. He staggered backward and fell against the wall. Flames crawled toward him. He screamed and smoke filled his throat, then the wind rushed past him. He looked up and saw the window.

"Mommy, Daddy," he whimpered. "Help me!"

The wall buckled as fingers of flame burst through it and licked their way up. He scrambled to his feet and climbed up on the window. A flame roared toward him, its heat singeing his hair. He cried out and let go, falling out the window to the soft leaves of the jungle floor, hurting his shoulder when he hit.

The heat from the house burned him. He shook with a jarring cough that cut into his chest like broken glass. He backed away. Tears streamed down his face and smoke burned his eyes. The whole house blossomed into a giant ball of angry orange and the trees around it exploded into smaller puffs of flame. Something cracked above him and a shower of sparks fell on his head. He burned his hands beating at it and ran screaming into the jungle.

A wall of crimson-orange raged into the night sky, driven by the wind. He ran, slipping and stumbling over roots. Vines and branches tore at his face and hair. When he was out of breath and dizzy from coughing, he looked back. Far off in the distance, the sky glowed. Where were Mommy and Daddy? He had never been alone out here, especially at night. The noises scared him.

He forced himself to walk until the fire became a shimmer on the horizon, then he found a clump of rocks that looked safe. Tired and numb, he felt as if all the fear had drained him of feeling. He climbed up into the rocks, burrowed under some leaves and cried himself to sleep.

The smell of smoke made him wake in a panic, but when he opened his eyes he felt no heat and saw no fire. Feeble sunbeams filtered through the haze of smoke and ash that blanketed the forest. His throat felt as if a coating of ash filled it. Deathly quiet hung over everything.

He climbed down from the safety of the rocks and stumbled through the haze, rubbing his eyes. The burning irritation stayed with him like the loss he felt inside. Hunger gnawed at his gut. He had no sense of direction, except away from the smoke toward cleaner air. Away from the compound.

By mid-morning, the smoke had thinned, but the forest remained dark and gloomy. He stumbled over roots and slippery trunks that crossed stagnant, bad smelling waters. Vines pulled at his pajamas, shredding them. Thorny branches tore at his skin.

He saw a dim light and followed it to a small clearing where huge blue butterflies fluttered in the hot air. He heard the buzz of bugs and the hum of bees. The sudden flash of a bright colored bird startled him. Beneath the din of the bugs he thought he heard another sound. Leaving the heat of the clearing, he headed off toward it.

His stomach and throat hurt and he felt weak. He tried eating some leaves, but they didn't taste good, so he spit them out. As he walked the forest gradually came back to life he saw and heard snakes, birds, and monkeys. Afraid to get too close, he avoided them, especially the snakes.

He saw bits of blue sky through the tree tops. The sounds grew louder, then he saw the river. The sky and wandering clouds cast floating shadows over the water and the brilliant sunlight on the sand hurt his eyes.

He took off his tattered pajamas and waded into the clear water, watching it darken from the soot that clung to him. He drank greedily and washed the pasty feeling from his mouth and throat. After drinking his fill, he rinsed the rest of the ash and smoke from himself. He felt much better, but his stomach still hurt.

Finding a high, flat rock to sleep on, he climbed up and stared at the swirling waters below to wait for the night. When the dark started, a big black cat came down to the water. After drinking, it looked up with huge yellow eyes and studied him before disappearing soundlessly back into the trees.

Hunger and frightening sounds kept him awake. He spent most of the night huddled on the rock crying.

More days and nights passed. He slept longer to escape the pain in his stomach. His head hurt, his body ached, and he felt lightheaded. With each new sunrise, he found it harder to climb up and down from the rock, until it became hard to walk. Finally, he crawled to the water's edge, collapsed and drifted in and out of awareness, spending more and more time in the black place.

In the midst of his delirium, he had the sensation of being lifted, then carried. Mommy had come for him, he thought. A billowing happiness filled him, but he had no strength to look up into the softness of her blue eyes, so he contented himself with snuggling against her.

She put him in bed and gave him small sips of juice and funny tasting drinks that made him stronger.

His breath caught when he opened his eyes and saw the painted face of an Indian staring down at him. He had never seen one like this. This man had feathers in his long black hair, dark eyes, and a necklace of sharp teeth and claws stuck inside a yellow rock. The points of the teeth and claws pointed out at four corners.

Erik thought the man was going to eat him until he sang an odd sounding song, blew smoke over him and splashed warm water on him. He held a shiny yellow rock and a rattle that he shook close to Erik's stomach. Taking a clear rock between his thumb and finger, he looked through it at Erik's stomach, then put it close to Erik's belly button, put his fist on it with his thumb up and sucked sharply through his thumb.

"Mommy," he cried in a hoarse whisper.

The man raised his hand and Erik flinched and stiffened, but the man's hand only stroked his hair gently. A huge grin broke across the man's face and his eyes smiled the same way Daddy's did. He gave Erik a furry monkey doll and left him alone.

Erik sat up in a hammock and looked around the long, smoke-blackened, dark house. Other Indians sat, talked, and moved around. An Indian boy who was bigger and older stared at him. Erik hoped that when he got better, they could play together until the boy gave him a mean look.

The man stayed close for the next few days, feeding him different food and drinks, blowing smoke over him, and splashing him with water while shaking a rattle. Erik couldn't eat much at first, but after awhile his hunger returned.

Sometimes he felt someone watching him. Looking up, he would see the boy peering around a corner, staring at him with eyes that weren't happy. Erik couldn't understand why.

He lay asleep one day holding the monkey doll when he felt it jerked away from him. His eyes opened and saw the Indian boy looming over him, fist raised. The fist didn't scare him as much as the wild look in the boy's eyes. Erik lay shaking as the boy ran out of the house with his only toy.

The Indian man came in later and said something Erik couldn't understand, but he knew by the man's gestures that he wanted to know what happened to the doll. Erik remembered the way the boy had looked at him and shook his head.

One day the man came in and gave him a small cloth like the one the other men and boys wore. After he helped Erik put it on, he took him by the hand and led him outside. A ring-shaped yard with a short trail leading away from it surrounded the front of the long house. Along the trail Erik saw pieces of old baskets, mats, small heaps of firewood and an old canoe. At the end of the path they came to a narrow stretch of riverbank.

The people that lived with him in the house took baths, women washed and soaked fruit and naked children ran to and fro, splashing in the water. A short distance from shore women cooked food in big pots over fires. A man came out of the woods carrying a dead monkey and a big bird over his shoulder. Other men worked on sharp sticks and long, hollow tubes. One man chopped away at the middle of a big log. No one had as many feathers or a necklace of sharp teeth and claws like his friend. From the way the other men acted, he knew his friend was in charge.

Everyone stopped what they were doing when they saw Erik. He realized that he was the only one with light skin and light hair. Embarrassed, he clutched the man's leg and hid behind him. The man laughed, patted his head, and spoke soft reassurances that Erik didn't understand.

The man called all the children together and had them line up. One by one they paraded in front of Erik. The boys smiled and touched him on the arm. The girls giggled and did the same. The last one in line was the boy with the angry eyes. He put his face right up to Erik's and glared.

Frightened, Erik stepped back. The man growled something and swatted the boy on the side of the head. The boy looked up with the same defiant stare. When the man raised his hand again, the boy turned his back and walked away. Erik looked up at the man and saw the hurt in his eyes. He yelled at the boy, then ruffled Erik's hair and spoke quietly to him.

CHAPTER THIRTY EIGHT

Despite the color of his skin, the men and women accepted Erik as one of their own and taught him their language and way of life. Namsaui, the man who had saved and adopted Erik named him Ebesoa, which meant to change, like a caterpillar into a butterfly. All the children played with him except for the boy with the mean eyes.

They called him Namaku which meant jaguar-lord. Everyone said he had a powerful spirit that needed to be tamed, and if he learned to control it, he would become their leader like his father Namsaui, the jaguar devourer. Namaku always watched Ebesoa from a distance, his dark eyes smoldering. If he saw Ebesoa playing alone, he took whatever the younger boy had and broke it, but when others were around he acted indifferent. Ebesoa soon learned to stay close to the other boys.

Their father Namsaui wore the sacred amulet which made him the head of the people. He treated Ebesoa like his own son and taught him the tribe's customs and language. Ebesoa learned fast and soon forgot the few English words he had learned. He longed to be friends with Namaku, but the other boy stayed sullen and withdrawn.

When Namaku turned eight, Namsaui took the two boys into the jungle to hunt. Ebesoa listened intently as his new father told him the habits of the animals.

"The forest may seem perfectly still." Namsaui made a sweeping gesture with his hand. "But the animals hide everywhere. A good hunter knows this. They hide behind fallen branches and between roots. They press their bodies to the ground or lie flat on overhanging branches." He pointed to a clump of brush, then to a branch. "They move quickly into the shadow of a bush, where they crouch and stop, watching for danger."

Ebesoa looked over at Namaku who stared off into the jungle. When he looked back to his father, the older man fixed his gaze on Namaku. "A good hunter always pays attention," he said.

Namaku continued staring off into the jungle. Namsaui picked up a clump of dirt and tossed it, hitting Namaku on the shoulder. The boy let out a startled shriek. Ebesoa burst into giggles until he saw the anger in his brother's eyes.

"That could have been a jaguar, ready to eat a boy who sleeps on his feet," Namsaui said sternly.

Namaku glared at Ebesoa, then stared at the ground.

Their father handed them each a bow and arrows. "I want you to go on a hunt of your own to see what you can find. You must return before darkness comes."

Ebesoa took the bow and crept off into the woods, anxious to please his father. He moved slowly, his senses poised for signs of life in the hiding places his father had shown him. It didn't take him long to spot a squirrel pressed against the side of a tree. He put an arrow into the bow, aimed and let it fly.

He thought he missed when the squirrel scampered up the tree a few steps, then it plummeted to the ground. Ebesoa stared at the lifeless animal at his feet. Part of him felt excited, knowing his father would be proud of him; another part felt sad at causing the squirrel's death. He didn't like to kill, but it was the way of the jungle. His family had to eat.

He picked the squirrel up by the tail and brought it back to his father. When Namsaui saw him, a smile spread across his face.

"You have done well." He ruffled Ebesoa's hair. "I did not expect you back so soon."

"Namaku isn't back?"

"We will give him a little more time, then we will look for him." Namsaui lowered his voice. "He does not listen when I speak. I am afraid he will not make a good hunter."

A short while later, Namsaui took Ebesoa back to the maloca where the rest of the tribe waited. He held the squirrel high above his head and told of Ebesoa's skill as a hunter. The women took the squirrel and praised him. Namsaui gave him a firm squeeze on the shoulder before turning down the path toward the jungle. "I must go find Namaku. The sun is falling quickly."

Ebesoa felt proud as the women fussed over him, but as the afternoon wore on, he worried about his father and brother. When no one was looking, he slipped out of the maloca and made his way down the path toward the jungle. He looked uncertainly up at the setting sun, clutching his bow for security. He had to find his father and brother.

He went to the spot where he had killed the squirrel and set off in the direction he thought Namaku had taken. Darkness crept in and Ebesoa started to turn back when he heard something. He listened carefully and worked his way toward it, recognizing it as the sound of Namaku crying.

He found his brother at the base of a large tree, a wild look in his eyes. When Namaku saw Ebesoa he hid his face and stopped.

"Are you all right?" Ebesoa asked.

Namaku sat up straight. His breath came in ragged sobs. He glared at Ebesoa, then put his head in his hands. "I got lost," he whispered between sobs.

Ebesoa sat down beside him. "I can take us back to the maloca."

Rage flashed in Namaku's eyes. "What do you know, Yellow Hair? You are not one of us. You are lost, just as I am." He put his head in his hands again and his body shook with sobs.

"I am not lost," Ebesoa said, his own anger flaring. "I came to look for you!" he said between gritted teeth. "It is dark. I will stay with you. We will find the maloca together in the morning."

Namaku looked up again, a puzzled expression on his face. In spite of his anger, Ebesoa felt sorry for him, so he sat down beside him. Soon Namaku slumped against Ebesoa, who struggled to stay awake and listen to the sounds of the night watching for signs of danger.

He started awake at the gentle touch of a hand and saw Namsaui standing over him. "I thought I left you at the maloca," he said.

Namaku jerked awake, eyes wide.

"It is all right, my sons," their father said. "The spirits of darkness haven't harmed you. My two young hunters are safe."

When they returned to the maloca, word spread about Ebesoa the brave and successful hunter and Namaku who had gotten lost and come back from the hunt without any game. The tribe whispered that the better hunter had gone back into the forest to find his brother.

The women giggled and the children laughed when they saw Namaku. Though the stories were true, Ebesoa didn't like them. He ached inside for his brother as though the other boy's pain were his own. For his part, Namaku told of how *he* had found Ebesoa crying in the woods and of how *he* had stayed with him during the night. Everyone laughed at his story and called him Namaku the jaguar cub.

When it came time for more hunting lessons, Namaku refused to go with Ebesoa, so Namsaui taught the two boys separately. Ebesoa listened to everything his father taught him and soon became a proficient hunter. Namaku learned slower and his skills were no match for Ebesoa's.

Time passed and Ebesoa grew in size and knowledge. The gap between him and his brother also grew, as did their mutual distrust. In the beginning, Ebesoa ignored his brother's provocations, but Namaku took every chance he could to ridicule and embarrass his brother. Eventually, everything they did became a competition.

Ebesoa sat alone in the jungle with Namsaui one day learning to hunt using arrows tipped with piranha teeth and the flying death. Bits of sunlight broke through the canopy. Ebesoa and Namsaui were painted in hunting colors to look invisible.

"Father," he said as he watched the older man prepare an arrow, "why does Namaku hate me?"

The old man looked up, his gaze steady. Ebesoa saw sadness in his eyes. He sighed and set his arrow to one side. "It is my fault. Namaku was my pride. He still is. He should be the leader of our people, but I have spoiled him. His mother died when he came into this world. In my sadness I gave him all my attention, but he has never been happy. He has the spirit of a powerful leader, but his anger blinds him."

Ebesoa thought of the mean things Namaku had done. Namsaui was right.

"I gave my complete love to him until that day I traveled as the eagle and saw you dying beside the stream. I went to you as a man and brought you to our people to save you from death. This required all my powers." He lowered his voice. "Namaku thought that I loved him no more. I tried to show him that my love for him is no less than before, but his jealousy has blinded him. He makes it hard to love him."

"I am sorry, father. I never meant to bring you unhappiness."

The old man's eyes widened. "Is that what you think? It is not true.

You have brought me great joy. It is sad to say, but I must speak the truth. You have given me greater joy than my own blood. Though he has sprung from my loins, I have grown to love you both equally." He looked away. "Is there not enough love for the two of you?"

Ebesoa didn't know what to say.

"In this world you are different. Your skin is light, your eyes are the color of the sky and your hair is the color of the sun, but you bleed the same as we and your spirit is gentle." His gaze went out of focus as if penetrating another reality. "In the other world, you are no different."

From that day forth, Ebesoa spent more time in the forest with his father. Namsaui had a knowledge of animals greater than anyone else in the tribe which puzzled him. When he asked about it, Namsaui smiled and told him that it was time to learn from the spirits of the plants who would teach him the secret of his animal brothers when he stood on the threshold of becoming a man.

CHAPTER THIRTY NINE

Namsaui sat cross-legged in the center of the maloca, Ebesoa on one side, Namaku on the other. "A warrior must have a deep interest in the myths and traditions of his people, a good memory for names and events, and a good singing voice."

Ebesoa knew by his father's somber tone that he was preparing them for an important test.

"He must be able to go for long times without food," Namsaui continued. "Above all he should shine with a strong inner light that makes itself visible to all that is in darkness and all that is hidden from ordinary knowledge. This light from the spirit world should show itself when he speaks, sings, or explains his or other's visions. When a warrior's explanations are not clear to the listener, his soul is not seen, it does not burn, and it does not shine. He must have clear and meaningful visions, his eyes must not be blurred. His hearing must be sharp."

"In the other world, a warrior has to move as a hunter," Ebesoa blurted. He glanced over at Namaku in time to catch his brother's frown.

Namsaui produced a small gourd container from his belt and a Y-shaped tube made from the leg-bones of a bird joined into one like smaller streams meeting to form a river. "Today we will look into the other side of the spirit world." He took a chunk of something red from the gourd and scraped bits of it off with a piece of rough white rock, making three piles, one bigger than the other two.

Taking the end of the Y with the two smaller tubes, he put it to his nose and mouth, inhaled sharp and handed it to Namaku who did the same. Ebesoa followed.

His nose burned and his eyes watered. Geometric patterns danced before his eyes, shifting and changing colors. He sensed the nearness of his father and brother experiencing the same thing. He thought of Namaku and the patterns grew stronger, as if invading his brain. He looked over at his brother and saw terror in his eyes. Ebesoa focused his thoughts and saw himself as a hunter, awake and aware.

The patterns shifted, making him feel as if he could see the inner workings of the lives of plants and animals. He looked over at Namaku and still saw fear, but this time he ignored it, sensing that he could share his brother's visions if he wished, but they had no order. He also understood that if he thought as a hunter, he could control his visions, unlike Namaku who let the visions control him.

Ebesoa smiled. The noises outside the maloca grew louder. He concentrated and discovered that he could project his hearing into the surrounding jungle and hear the animals moving through the trees. His enhanced perceptions showed him how his father knew so much about the animals.

His experience lasted until dark, diminishing as the light of the sun faded behind the trees. Ebesoa felt lightness in his heart and thankfulness for the privilege of glimpsing the spirit world.

When it ended Namsaui quizzed the two boys, smiling as Ebesoa told of his vision of the inner workings of plants and animals. His features darkened when Namaku spoke of chaos and destruction.

"If, under the influence of the spirits, a warrior confuses his waking life with those of his visions," Namsaui said, "he should not do evil. One day you must go to the other world and move as a hunter, seeking the sacred animal. The one who envisions the sacred animal will become the leader of the people." He fingered the amulet hanging from his neck. "With the help of this power object, his true powers will awaken in his thirtieth season, but it must be sought with a pure heart. Power selects its bearer, not the other way around."

The two boys looked at each other. Namaku's eyes narrowed. Ebesoa stared back for a moment, then shook his head and smiled.

In the months that followed, their father took them into the jungle and taught them how to find sacred plants; particularly the Holy Flower of the North Star, and the Flying Death. Namsaui said it would be a special day when they sought out the Vision Vine because it was the plant that really gave them entry into the world of their animal brothers. Yajé would let them see the world through the jaguar, the animal lord.

When he heard this, Namaku puffed out his chest. "I am Namaku, the jaguar lord. He and I are one. The power will seek me."

His boast seemed true. Namaku excelled in finding and preparing the plants. His father's pride was obvious. Ebesoa did almost as well, but Namaku had a better grasp of the plant world and reminded Ebesoa of it every chance he got. Secretly relieved that his brother found something that he excelled at, Ebesoa didn't mind, especially when he saw that it brought his father happiness.

One morning Namsaui woke them early saying, "Today is the day you will learn the secret of your animal brothers. You will have to pass through the doorway into the spirit world many times before the final ceremony where you will hunt your visions and meet your spirit animals, then you will be ready to die as boys and become men."

Ebesoa could hardly contain his excitement. They had spent months learning about many plants, except the Vision Vine. One by one they used the other plants in small doses and received glimpses of the other world. Today they would go to it and learn about the jaguar, then it would only be a matter of time before they participated in the battle of the two spirits.

The brother of the sacred animal would be the leader of the people. Namaku, the jaguar lord, was the brother of the jaguar and Ebesoa felt sure the jaguar was his sacred animal. Namaku would have the vision and would be the leader of the people.

The thought of his brother in that role made Ebesoa uneasy. Namaku cared little for the traditions, yet he had a mastery of the plants. The tests were *never* wrong. The battle of the two spirits would decide. If Namaku became the leader, Ebesoa would accept his brother's rule, but he knew his life would become more difficult. Namaku did not know kindness and cared only for himself. Ebesoa could only put his faith in the wisdom of tradition.

Namsaui took them into the jungle and led them to a long, ascending trail that ended at the top of a small hill where he stopped and pulled at some leafy vines hanging down in profusion from the trees. He broke off a piece and chewed. A thoughtful look crossed his face. He spit out the splinters and pulled at another vine. A shower of dry leaves and ants fell over them. They all laughed, slapping each other's shoulders and thighs.

When their mirth subsided, Namsaui selected woody vines, directing Ebesoa to clear off the leaves and small branches while Namaku cut off finger thick stems that he bundled together. Each time he came to a tree, Namsaui chewed a piece of a stem before he pulled down the required quantity.

"This is guano Yajé." He showed Ebesoa and Namaku the stems he had taken from high above his head which were light brown. The surface of the bark had raised ridges. Other vines, taken from the height of his head looked brown with light spots and smooth bark. He called this "animal Yajé". A third vine taken at ground level he called "head Yajé". It had dark colored stems that were knotty and twisted.

When they had three bundles, Namsaui took them back down the trail, but instead of going to their maloca, he led them to a part of the jungle they had never been to before where a smaller maloca lay hidden among a group of trees. Namsaui cleaned a wooden trough that hung outside the door and broke stems into smaller pieces which he threw into the trough. Taking a club of heavy redwood, he beat the stems with the blunt end, using heavy rhythmical blows, occasionally breaking into a chant.

He pounded them for a long time, poured cold water over the pulpy mass and picked out woody splinters, then took a small gourd-cup, filled it with water and put a few fibers of the shredded vine into it, smiling when the water turned a cloudy white.

"It is starchy! It is good! We shall see many visions!"

By the time he finished, the sun had set and darkness filled the maloca. Namsaui took a painted piece of pottery hanging from a rafter and cleaned it. Murmuring and chanting as he worked, he walked along the walls of the maloca, chanting and gesturing with a small torch and lighting others before putting the clay pot on the floor. He grabbed a large circular basket, held it over the pot and filled a gourd-cup from the trough, pouring the contents over the sieve so the strained liquid dripped into the pot.

The three of them painted their legs and arms by dipping small circular stamps into berry juice and rolling them over their skin, leaving bands of designs, then Namsaui took out a long wooden box and prepared himself.

He looked frightening, but more than that, he stood powerful and majestic arrayed in a way that only the spiritual leader of the tribe could -- the one man of all the people who had become the brother of the sacred animal.

He wore a jaguar skin and a headdress of claws turned upward with a necklace of teeth that dwarfed his amulet. Around his waist he carried bags of dark, spotted jaguar fur which held special herbs, magic stones, and the tube made of hollow bird legs. He kept the red vision powder in a tubular jaguar bone closed on one end with pitch and on the other with a wooden stopper.

Namsaui took a small bowl of darker berry juice and painted his face with black spots that resembled jaguar pelt marks, then sat the boys in front of him.

"Today you will go through the doorway into the world of the animal spirits where the jaguar is the lord. This will prepare you for the day when you die as boys and become men. You must seek the jaguar spirit first. He will allow you to move about in his world. You must move as the hunter. Both eyes open. Awake. Always watching. Always listening."

He dipped a small gourd into the pot, withdrew it, drank quickly and dipped again, handing the gourd to Namaku whose face contorted when he swallowed. Ebesoa drank last, gagging at the bitterness.

Namsaui chanted and made jaguar sounds as they passed the gourd. His chants grew louder with each drink until he stood and danced, moving like a jaguar, singing songs to its spirit. Namaku and Ebesoa imitated him, pausing every few minutes to drink from the gourd.

Ebesoa soon felt giddy. His stomach knotted and his body grew slippery with sweat until he vomited. When his nausea passed, he felt euphoric. Sitting down, he enjoyed the sensation while Namaku vomited beside him.

The fluttering red of the torches filled the maloca, their flickers turning to patterns and the patterns to colors; first white, then a hazy, smoky blue that increased in intensity with each pulse of the torches. Ebesoa closed his eyes and let the visions wash over him. Bright light shot out in both directions, then straight up, making a doorway of light. He had the sensation of floating, as if something gentle lifted him through the door, then up and out the roof of the maloca. He saw Namaku floating beside him.

He closed his eyes and opened them, finding himself in the jungle, Namaku still with him. The jungle seemed more alive than he had ever seen it. A low growl filled his ears, startling him. Remembering his father's imitations, he looked into the undergrowth in front of him expecting to see Namsaui. His heart jerked when two huge yellow eyes stared out and a massive jaguar rose in front of them.

Namaku smiled and Ebesoa felt too scared to move. Namaku held his arms wide and the jaguar came forward, opening its mouth, then leaping forward, swallowing the two boys in darkness.

Ebesoa rushed forward through the darkness before his vision returned in a flash of illumination. The jungle around him looked sharper, with better clarity than he had imagined possible. He heard a noise and felt his ears moving forward. Every sound came distinct with greater volume. His smell became acute and magnified. The jaguar hadn't really swallowed him. He had *become* the jaguar.

So had Namaku.

Ebesoa sensed his brother with him, sharing the magnificent perceptions of their host. Enthralled with his new power, Ebesoa willed himself forward, but Namaku's thoughts overpowered him, seizing control of the cat. Ebesoa tried to reassert his will, but his brother's thoughts pushed him down as if trapping him in some lower part of the cat's mind, making him experience what happened without control; forced to participate as a powerless observer.

The jaguar lord had asserted himself.

Ebesoa fought panic, dreading the consequences of his brother's control. Helpless to resist, he forced himself to remain calm and watch and wait like a hunter the way his father had taught him.

Together they moved through the forest, saturated in the rich textures of their heightened perceptions. Swift and powerful limbs carried them. The sense of superiority over the other animals giving them a wide berth felt heady.

A river bank loomed in front of them. Crouching, they listened and smelled the air, sorting through the musty rot of the riverbank for the scent of prey. The sound of chattering monkeys came to them first. They crept forward, belly close to the ground, taking in the scent. Saliva flowed to the cat's mouth.

Ebesoa felt a forbidden thrill that frightened him. He "felt" his brother's thoughts. Namaku liked this part. Ebesoa didn't. The sound of the monkeys came closer.

Muscles coiled, then leaped, silently propelling them to the top of a rock. Two monkeys below splashed in the water, drinking and bathing.

Another rush of saliva.

They pressed themselves close to the rock, rear haunches moving from side to side, claws extended, fangs pushed forward, muscles bunching.

A high pitched scream ripped through the jungle as claw and fang buried themselves in soft fur. Bones crunched and the second monkey fled, its cries piercing the night air. The lone victim struggled and flopped from side to side, its hot, salty blood jetting. The jaguar bit again, closing its jaws on the monkey's neck, snapping it.

Ebesoa took it all in, torn between the delight of the cat's fulfillment, horrified with the savagery, not only of the beast, but of his brother.

The monkey twitched as life flowed from it and the cat carried its warm carcass up to the branch of a tree where it devoured its remains.

Ebesoa couldn't deny the cat's satisfaction, but his human side felt shame at taking part in the killing, yet he knew he had been helpless to act. Exhaustion swept through him and he drifted. His perceptions blurred, his mind grayed and he floated…

…until he saw a flickering redness that made him think of blood. He blinked and recognized the walls of the maloca bathed in red. Shifting patterns danced before him. He turned his head and saw the red flame of the torch cast its light on the walls. His father sat cross-legged in front of him, eyes closed. Namaku sat beside him licking his lips, a catlike smile filling his face.

CHAPTER FORTY

In preparation for the battle of the two spirits, Namsaui took his sons to the hidden maloca many times to drink of the bitter fluid of the vision vine. On the day of the battle, only one would seek the sacred animal.

Each time they went to the maloca and drank, they had visions. Both saw the jaguar. Namaku went to it every time before it would swallow Ebesoa, making him subject to Namaku's vicious killing sprees. Ebesoa always tried to free himself, but once inside the cat, he became subject to his brother's domination.

Namaku knew Ebesoa didn't like the experience. He took pleasure in forcing the smaller boy to participate in the slaughter and when their father wasn't around, he teased Ebesoa about it.

After the effects of the vine wore off, Namsaui always quizzed them about their visions. When they gave their accounts, the old man would shake his head, saying, "You must go to the spirit world again and see beyond the jaguar."

Ebesoa knew he had to escape the jaguar to see beyond it. He had to resist with all his will *before* the jaguar could swallow him. In spite of his brother's taunts, he would exercise his will the next time Namsaui took them to the hidden maloca.

Two nights later, they went to the maloca and performed the ritual as they had before. On this night, Namaku's rendition of the jaguar's growl sent a chill fluttering down Ebesoa's spine.

The roar sounded real.

The patterns and colors came and the door of light opened,

followed by the sensation of floating. Once in the surreal jungle of the other world, Ebesoa saw the jaguar. Namaku ran to it as he had every time and the jaguar swallowed him, locking its gaze on Ebesoa.

His legs felt rubbery and his heart thudded as if his ribs were a cage holding back his own jaguar. Keeping his eyes pinned to the cat, he resisted with his mind as it slunk toward him. It came within inches of his face and stopped, its yellow eyes studying him intently. Ebesoa felt an overwhelming urge to go to it, but he held his ground. He would not let Namaku rule his experience.

The cat opened its mouth and let out a thunderous roar that shook Ebesoa and the ground beneath him. He closed his eyes, thinking that it really had been thunder.

When he opened them the jaguar had gone. A spinning blackness took its place. Panic gripped him as he sailed through the air. For an instant he thought of a bird in flight…

…and in the next moment his vision had an acuity that exceeded that of the jaguar. Spreading his wings, he caught an updraft and soared, laughing in delight as he dove and soared again. He had never known freedom such as this. He saw a river, sailed low and skimmed its surface until he came to a calm pool. Arching his wings, he lit on the branch of a tree to study himself in the water's reflection and saw speckled feathers on his chest, a short, hooked bill, and strong talons.

A hawk.

He yelped with excitement, his outburst flying from him as a shrill cry. Flapping powerful wings, he took to the air once again and flew as high as he dared to study the minutiae of the jungle below.

When his perceptions faded, he flew upward and hurtled toward the moon. Spiraling lights filled his vision as the sensation of flying apart overwhelmed him.

In the next moment, he was on the floor of the maloca, spirals spinning dully through his brain like dying embers from a cooking fire. The smiling face of his father loomed over him.

"You cried like the hawk!" Namsaui said excitedly. "Have you soared with him?"

Ebesoa smiled. He *had* soared. High above the jaguar. He looked into his father's eyes and nodded, then heard a roar and hiss from his brother, who rolled on the floor.

"Namaku is still with the jaguar," Namsaui said. His face brightened. "We will wait for him to return, then you will tell us of the hawk."

Namaku came out of his trance a short while later, hissing and pawing at the floor. When his eyes fluttered open he frowned at his brother. "You did not hunt with the jaguar. Is his magic too strong for you?"

Namsaui spoke before Ebesoa could answer. "His magic is stronger than the jaguar's. He has gone beyond the jaguar's world to fly with the hawk."

Namaku's frown deepened. "Tell us how this came to be," he said.

Ebesoa told them how he had resisted the jaguar and how the cat had roared and shook the ground with thunder that sent him flying into the air.

Namsaui stopped him. "You have made an ally of the Thunder-Spirit." He clenched his fists and shook them. "A warrior can turn into thunder. The roar of The Thunder-Spirit is a brother to the growl of the jaguar."

Ebesoa told of how he flew over the forest and saw his reflection in a pool of water. Namsaui urged him to seek the Thunder-Spirit in all his visions so he could move through the forest with different animals. Namaku sat quietly until his father turned to him.

"You must break free of the jaguar's magic like your brother," he said solemnly. "Give yourself to the Thunder-Spirit. Let him carry you to other animals."

"Only by moving through all the animals in the jungle can you reach a full understanding of your animal brothers," he said. "To know their spirits is the path to becoming The Master of the Animals. The jaguar is the guardian to the door of the other world. You must go through him to reach the others. The only way to do this is to become thunder."

In the days that followed, Ebesoa went to different animals with each new vision. He couldn't control what animals he went to, but he seemed to have an affinity for birds. In the beginning Namaku stayed with the jaguar, but eventually he too began moving through different animals. Though he experienced many different creatures, he spent most of his time as snakes and other predators, particularly the jaguar.

First Ebesoa, then Namaku began dreaming their visions and becoming different animals each night. Namsaui taught them how to sleep with their heads in different directions to change what animals they became, but neither boy acquired full control over any. As the vividness of their dreams increased, their trips to the secret maloca and its rituals decreased.

One day Namsaui announced that they were close to becoming men. They had to prepare themselves for the battle of the two sides of the spirit. Each would meet his spirit animal who would show them the path, but only one would have the vision of The Sacred Animal. He would be the one to wear the amulet and become the leader of the people in the thirtieth season of his life.

They didn't eat any meat for days and days, only thin soups, bits of cassava bread, and manioc starch with fish. Their visions grew stronger. Ebesoa tried to control what animals he could go to, but the process still seemed random.

Namaku didn't assert himself. "I am the Jaguar Lord," he said. "The power will seek me." Clearly, he thought himself superior because of his skin color and made that point repeatedly whenever his father was not around, but Ebesoa remembered his father's words. "In this world you are different from us. Your skin is light, your eyes are the color of the sky, and your hair is the color of the sun, but you bleed the same as we and your spirit is gentle. In the other world you are no different."

Ebesoa knew the time for the ritual had come when Namsaui and the other men filled the maloca one evening as the sun fell behind the treetops in a blaze of red. The unannounced appearance of the painted men with ornaments and weapons made him uneasy. One of them beat a drum, stomped his foot and shook a rattle. Others joined in, playing music on fifes, flutes, and other instruments of reed, bone, and turtle shell.

Namaku smiled and crossed his arms. The drums boomed deeper and the men formed a circle around the boys. One of the older men said something and the women scattered into the surrounding jungle.

When the women were gone the men produced four pairs of horns from hiding places. They sat in a semi-circle and began playing mournful notes. The older men took out their ceremonial feathers and selected brilliant ruffs which they tied to the mid-section of the longer horns.

Four men danced through the maloca, blowing the decorated horns as they advanced and retreated with short steps. Two of them danced out the door with their horns raised to the sky, then returned. The expanding and contracting feather ruffs gave off beautiful bursts of translucent color against the light of the torches.

A moment later Namsaui appeared dressed in red carrying a strangely shaped clay jar. Ebesoa and Namaku sat obediently as their father made them drink a thick brown bitter liquid from tiny round gourds. Namaku vomited after his first drink. Though he felt sick, Ebesoa held his down. The sound of the drums and horns diminished while Namsaui stayed in the center of the maloca, bowing, advancing, and retreating.

The older men outfitted themselves with their finest headbands, resplendent with guacamayo feathers, egret plumes, oval pieces of the russet skin of the howler monkey, disks of armadillo hide, loops of monkey-hair, quartzite cylinders, and jaguar tooth belts. They formed a swaying, dancing semi-circle, each putting his right hand on his neighbor's shoulder while shifting and stomping together.

Namsaui led, blowing tobacco smoke on his companions from a huge cigar in an engraved ceremonial fork. His long, polished rattle-lance vibrated. The group chanted familiar sounds as their voices rose, fell, and mingled with the booming tones of the horns.

Namsaui's voice rose above them all. "Behold the wonder of the sacred vision. The battle of the two sides of the spirit. You will meet your spirit animal and he will show you the path. He who has the vision is the brother of the sacred animal. The one who must lead."

Ebesoa's vision grew hazy until a flurry of colors blossomed before him. Namaku glared at him, his expression angry and malevolent. The Jaguar Lord. Ebesoa accepted the fact that Namaku would go to the jaguar -- the ruler of the jungle -- surely the sacred animal. A sick feeling hung in the pit of his stomach at the thought of his brother ruling, followed by the sense of a massive boulder lowered onto his shoulders. The winds came and carried him up out of the maloca, through the door of light and over the trees.

He saw the jaguar prowling. It looked over at him and he froze. His heart fluttered like a frightened bird. The cat's gaze looked angry. Namaku. It growled and moved away.

An anaconda dropped from a branch above him, its head inches from his face. It frightened him, but he felt more afraid of giving in to fear. The snake opened its mouth as if to swallow him. He felt compelled to give himself to it, but something held him back. To do so would be a mistake. The sacred animal must lead. Show him the path.

The serpent drew back, its eyes glittering like sunlight off the surface of polished stones. Ebesoa started toward it, then stopped. The snake opened its mouth wider and slithered toward him. Ebesoa wanted to give himself, free himself, but he closed his eyes and willed himself not to move.

When he opened them he saw a snake he had never seen before. The back of its head flared wide and flat as it reared back, about to strike. If he gave in to the fear, its strike would be ineffective. If he resisted -- he closed his eyes again and heard a fluttering, then a flapping. He opened them and the fluttering filled his vision. An eagle swooped down out of the trees to catch the serpent's tail in its beak. It rose and took the writhing serpent high above the jungle.

Ebesoa's heart swelled as he soared with the eagle and became the bird, gliding on the wind, a snake in his beak that struck at him. He flipped sideways. It missed and struck again. He dodged. Fear gripped him, but he felt power from the eagle's body.

The snake wrapped itself around him and pinned his wings. He plummeted, biting deep, claws digging at the cold skin of his antagonist. The snake tightened its grip and he fell faster. The snake flipped from side to side as the ground rushed toward them. At the last moment the snake loosened its grip and Ebesoa spread his wings, passing within inches of the ground, flapping hard, catching the wind, rising. Rising.

The snake struck at him again. He dodged and flew higher toward a distant peak. When the snake stopped moving, he made one last mighty flap of his wings and let the serpent fall, tumbling through the air to its rocky death below.

Elated, he soared and the breeze took him again, carrying him until he became formless, riding the wind. His world grayed and in that moment he knew. He could choose. Any animal he wished. Simply by overcoming fear and asserting his will. It didn't matter that Namaku had become the brother of the sacred animal. Ebesoa didn't care. He could soar with *his* brother.

The eagle.

CHAPTER FORTY ONE

R ed fingers of light from the torches flickered lower while the first pink beams of the coming day painted the walls of the maloca in fading red that bled into pink. In spite of feeling worn and sleepy, Ebesoa's new knowledge buoyed his spirits. Beside him sat Namaku, eyes narrowed, arms crossed. Proud. Defiant. The Jaguar Lord.

Namsaui sat before them. The rest of the men made a semi-circle behind them.

"Tell us of your visions," Namsaui said eyeing Namaku, then Ebesoa. "Tell us of your battles.”

"I am the Jaguar Lord." Namaku pounded his chest. "I did not need to struggle. The jaguar is more powerful than any creature of the forest. The jaguar is the sacred animal. I went to him and claimed his power as my own."

A pained look pinched Namsaui's features. None of the other men made a sound. The silence felt oppressive. "You did not engage in battle?" he said incredulously.

Namaku shook his head.

Namsaui turned to Ebesoa, eyes questioning. "And what of you, my son? Did you not struggle with the two sides of your soul?"

Ebesoa stared at the ground, embarrassed that he had experienced fear. "I saw the jaguar and was afraid," he said quietly. "My heart felt like a frightened bird."

"A hummingbird," Namaku sneered. "You fear the power of the jaguar. You have a hummingbird's heart." He laughed.

"Silence!" Namsaui barked, then "Compared to its body the hummingbird's heart is the biggest in the animal world." A murmur passed among the men. Namsaui looked back to Ebesoa. "Go on," he said, lowering his voice.

"As soon as the jaguar went on his way," Ebesoa said, looking everywhere but at his father, "an anaconda dropped from the trees and opened his mouth to swallow me. I wanted to give myself to him, but I knew if I did I would give myself to the fear so I closed my eyes." He took a slow breath. "When I opened them a snake I had never seen before rose in front of me."

Another murmur passed among the men. Namsaui silenced them with a wave of his hand.

"I could not move," Ebesoa said. "And then I knew. I did not have to give myself to him. I could choose -- and in my heart I wished for the guidance of the sacred animal." He felt the eyes of all the men on him. "And then I heard a fluttering." He remembered the eagle, smiled, and sat up straight. "My brother came down from the sky, took the snake in his beak and carried it away." His voice rose in volume like the flight of the bird. "I flew with him and together we fought the snake. I knew I had not contacted the sacred animal, but it did not matter. The eagle was my brother."

The crowd broke into excited chatter, making Ebesoa feel uneasy. Looking back, he saw a small sea of smiling faces. Somebody patted him on the shoulder. He turned back and saw his father gaze upward, hands spread, a beatific smile filling his face. Tears spilled down his cheeks. The soft pink of the morning light lit his features as if adding to his joy.

"The eagle *is* the sacred animal," he said in a trembling voice. "*You* are the brother of the sacred animal. The one who must lead." He took the amulet from his neck and placed it on Ebesoa's. "You have won the battle of the two sides of the spirit."

A swell of confusing emotion swept over Ebesoa. "But I thought…" He looked over at Namaku who sat with his mouth gaping in surprise. The red from the dying torches flickered across his face like boiling water. Ebesoa saw his mouth set into a thin line and his eyes narrowed into the defiant stare Ebesoa knew from their childhood. Mad eyes.

A tremor shook him.

The men of the tribe swarmed around him, blocking his view as they congratulated him. When he could see again, Namaku had gone.

The women returned and prepared a celebration. Overwhelmed by all that happened, Ebesoa went along with the festivities, drinking cashiri beer with the men and sharing food with the women. Namaku remained conspicuously missing from the festivities. No one spoke of his absence.

The tribe fell quiet when he entered the maloca late in the afternoon carrying a gourd rattle. He went straight to Ebesoa and placed the rattle in his hands.

"You are the seeker of visions." He bowed his head. "You have won the battle of the two sides of your spirit and have become one with the sacred animal. You are the new leader of our people. I want you to have my rattle."

Ebesoa stared down at the rattle made from a large gourd, decorated with incised designs and didn't know what to say. The handle was made of hard reddish wood and had an irregular shape that branched out like a hand. His heart tightened and tears came to his eyes.

"Thank you, brother."

Namsaui hugged them both. "My sons," he said. "My two young men. May this moment stay in your hearts."

Namaku joined his father and brother, all drinking cashiri beer from the same gourd. When they drained it, Namaku went to the trough and brought a cup back for each of them. The rest of the men drank a toast to Namaku's gesture and the celebration continued, louder than before.

A short while later, Namsaui excused himself, saying he needed to rest. The rituals and celebration had tired him. The other men teased him about becoming an old man. He laughed and left the maloca carrying his hammock.

Ebesoa realized that he too felt tired. It had been a long night. He tried to stay awake as long as he could, but he could not keep his eyes open and his arms and legs felt weak. Too much cashiri beer, he thought. He staggered out of the maloca amidst jokes about acting like his father.

He knew Namsaui had gone to sleep away from the noise, so he set off through the manioc fields heading in the direction of the secret maloca. Walking grew difficult. He pushed himself, but his legs faltered, then refused to respond, causing him to fall forward, face first into the undergrowth of the jungle floor.

He tried to push himself up, but his arms were as limp as his legs, reminding him of the way monkeys acted when hit by a dart tipped with the flying death. Something more than cashiri beer had taken him over. His breathing came harder, his eyelids drooped, and he thought of death as darkness crept into his mind.

He heard the cries of macaws and parrots off in the distance as his senses dimmed. Weaverbirds and hummingbirds flitted to and fro. Squirrels and mice scampered around him.

The flying death, he thought. He didn't have to die. Fixing his gaze on a mouse burrowing beneath the root of a bush in front of him he focused his thoughts until the weight of his body seemed to float away and his senses blurred. A moment later he became the mouse, looking up at the huge unconscious form of his body.

He scurried over to the base of a bush and gnawed at a leaf. When it fell, he dragged it back to where his tongue lolled out of the mouth of his listless human body. A string of drool trailed to the ground.

Working the end of the leaf into his human mouth, he pushed at it until the body shook and gagged. He scampered backward when the body convulsed and a stream of vomit shot forth from the open mouth, barely missing him.

That's all I can do, he thought, running through the jungle watching for predators. I hope I saved myself. I have to get to the other maloca. Father is in danger.

He found Namsaui's inert body lying on a hammock in the maloca. His tiny mouse heart fluttered as he worked his way up the wall and onto the rope suspending the hammock. When he reached his father's head, he stopped next to the old man's nose. A faint breath ruffled his fur.

If he could only get his father to spit up what he -- a low growl made his fur stand on end, then he jumped, more from instinct than thought. Half his body slipped through the hammock. Pulling himself up, he burrowed into the hair on his father's neck. The massive head of a jaguar loomed into view. A clump of feathers stuck out of its mouth. Eagle feathers. And the rattle. The rattle that Namaku had…

The cat dropped the feathers and rattle on Namsaui and extended a single claw. In one swipe a clean slice opened across Namsaui's neck. Blood flowed, covering everything in red. Ebesoa stifled the urge to cry out. The cat pushed his father's head aside and Ebesoa looked up into its huge yellow eye.

The jaguar opened its mouth and sharp teeth closed in, piercing skin and fur. Ebesoa squealed in agony and willed himself back to his human form. Darkness swept in...

Fluttering. The beat. He flew with the eagle. Protected. He tried to remember what happened but sensed only sadness. His thoughts came vague and disoriented. Fluttering. The rhythm. Darkness until he opened his eyes and studied the undergrowth in front of his face where he had tripped and fallen. His heart punched his ribs and thumped in his ears. His breath came short and hard. The heaviness of the air pressed on his chest.

Thin shafts of sunlight pierced the dense canopy and streamed down through heavy mist, diffusing their light on the jungle's matted floor. Huge ferns hung low, bowed in silent witness to the oppressive surroundings. Bugs crawled in front of him watched by the single unblinking eye of a lizard.

Its tongue lashed out in a blur of movement. Ebesoa shuddered, remembering how it felt to be the prey.

The thought of staying where he had fallen flitted through his mind with the hope that his pursuer might pass him by, but he knew better.

The jaguar was a skilled hunter.

Even now it probably stalked him.

He pushed a tangle of shoulder length blond hair away from his sweaty forehead and tried to remember how he had come to be prey. A haze clouded his thoughts as though the dense, early morning mist had seeped into his mind. He didn't know where he was, who he was, where he had come from, or where he was trying to go.

The mournful cry of a jungle bird jolted him. Sensing the nearness of his pursuer, he pushed himself up and stumbled through the undergrowth. A wave of dizziness washed through him. Vines whipped his face and tripped him. Startled birds flew from their nests. He slipped on a rock and fell again at the base of a tree.

He crawled, then stood on trembling legs and wiped stinging sweat from his eyes. Looking down at his hands he saw blood smeared with sweat, then the amulet. A vague sense of memory flickered before another dizzy spell took him. He tried hard to think. Nothing. Only danger.

He spotted an orange glow at the same moment he felt the eyes on him. A cold, violent shiver wracked his whole body. He turned, his head inching toward the jungle behind him until his widened eyes locked with the stare of a black jaguar.

Motionless, it crouched, close to seven feet long with short massive limbs and a large head. The cat bared its fangs and hissed, then dropped lower, preparing to leap.

Ebesoa knew the end had come and braced himself for the inevitable frenzy of claws and fangs. He turned toward the orange glow he had glimpsed. Fire? Men? Could he reach them? Better to die trying.

He gave his own savage animal scream and bolted toward the glow. The jaguar closed the gap behind him, cutting the distance quickly. Ebesoa braced for its claws raking his back and its hot breath on his neck. Its teeth would sink into his flesh finding their mark at the base of his skull, cracking his spine like a twig.

The cat snarled and leaped. Its shadow hovered above him and blocked out the forest for an eternal moment before hitting with an explosive crack. Ebesoa fell forward under the weight, his head bounced off a rock and a bright flash filled his mind.

Another explosive crack jolted him. Wetness peppered his forehead. Rain. Light pressure on his chest.

Erik opened his eyes and another peal of thunder rocked Tahquitz peak. An eagle sat on his chest, calmly gazing at him.

As soon as their eyes met, the eagle flapped its mighty wings and took to the air, rising high above the circle of rocks where Erik lay, as if lifting the invisible shroud that had hung over his entire adult life.

His body shook. His chest swelled and his tears mixed with the rain. He smiled in gratitude as his brother the eagle soared above him.

Erik Ebesoa Simpson remembered.

CHAPTER FORTY TWO

Namaku.

His Indian brother had come from the jungle and now ran rampant through the High Sierras in the form of a jaguar that killed and butchered people so he could draw Erik out and finish what he had started so many years ago by invading Erik's dreams and rubbing his face in the grisly killings with the same perverse pleasure he showed in his youth.

His real parents had died in a fire. He barely remembered them, but he did remember the two fathers who'd adopted and loved him as if he'd been their own; Namsaui his Indian father and Phineas his Scottish father. Namaku had murdered them both, as well as his friend, Lieutenant Mitchell. Namaku the Jaguar Lord, the hunter, the butcher-murderer had taken away everyone Erik loved and had almost killed him more than once.

His brother understood only one set of standards he had inherited from spending so much time with the jaguar. The strong hunted the weak and killed for pleasure and power. He couldn't understand the language of reason. He only understood the language of death.

There were no alternatives to stopping him. Erik had to deal with his brother on terms he could understand and Erik was the only one capable of speaking his language.

He climbed out of his sleeping bag and stretched. His thoughts felt curiously detached, as if a delay between the impulse to think and the actual thought slowed them. His body felt fragile and weak, his throat dry. How long had he been up here? His legs felt stiff and brittle. Forcing himself to walk gingerly, he felt like one good fall would shatter his body.

He looked up to the sky and felt light rain pelting his face. The eagle had disappeared. Leaden clouds rolled in, blanketing the sky in darkened turmoil. A roll of thunder shook the mountain as if urging him on. When he felt he could trust his legs, he packed up his gear and made his way down through mist covered trails while thunder growled in the distance. The heavy fog and thunder backdrop combined with his detached mental state made everything surreal, as if he were still in the midst of his vision. It wasn't until he came to his car at Humber Park that he felt sure he had come back to the real world.

He called Nicole while driving down to Idyllwild.

"Where have you been?" she said angrily. "Are you all right? You had me worried sick!"

"How long have I been gone?"

"Two days. I was getting ready to call the police. Everyone's looking for you. Fritz is frantic. Some jerk from the Forestry Service named Schmitten has been looking for you." Her tone softened. "Are you all right?"

"Sorry, but I had to do this alone. I know what's happening. I've -- I've relived my past. I know everything."

"You remember?"

"I have some unfinished business with a jaguar. I don't have time to explain right now. I'll tell you everything when there's time. Can you call Fritz for me?"

"Sure."

"Tell him I'll meet him at the zoo this afternoon."

"I've thought about you so much, I'm starting to think like you," she said. "I stopped at the zoo the other day to talk to Fritz and I could swear that an animal he was treating stared at me as if it was human. Fritz laughed and said it looked that way because it was sedated."

"Listen," Erik said. "I'm sure he's right, but I think it would be a good idea if you stayed away from the zoo. I'll call you first chance I get."

Erik went to the Idyllwild ranger station and had them relay a message to Schmitten, letting him know he would be back up to help with the hunt as soon as he took care of some important business at the zoo.

After a quick stop for food and a change of clothes, Erik met Fritz at the zoo and gave him the details of his discovery. Fritz listened wide-eyed, then took Erik's hand and pumped it.

"Congratulations on discovering your past." His voice lowered. "Call if you need me. I don't care where I am or what time of day it is. If there is a problem, I am ready to help. You do what you have to. Neither one of us can feel comfortable as long as that brute is running loose in the mountains."

After Fritz left, Erik took a walk through the compound, knowing that the musky scent of the compound's inhabitants would relax him. When he reached the back of the building he saw that a new shipment had come in. One of the smaller animals sleeping in its shipping cage gave him an idea. He picked up the cage and it looked up at him. Erik stuck his finger between the wires and a mongoose nuzzled it. He smiled and brought the cage back to his office.

Pulling out the cot, he lay with his hands behind his head, trying to figure a way to find his brother in the mountains. Namaku had to be close to the jag. If he could find the cat's lair, his brother wouldn't be far. Smell was the best way. Another bear, only this time, he wouldn't let it get killed.

He turned the cot, oriented it, and held the image of a black bear in his mind while focusing his thoughts north toward the search party in King's Canyon. A short while later he slid off into deep sleep...

...opening his eyes to the sights and sounds of the Sierras at night. The myriad scents of humans, campfires, and sweat overwhelmed him. Beneath them he sensed the normal scents of the wilderness, and undercutting them the lingering traces of the intruder.

He circled the human camp, giving it a wide berth. The malevolent scent of the foreigner grew stronger the higher up the slope he went. Lumbering to the top, he crested a hill and caught the cat's smell coming to him on a light breeze. He worked his way down into a draw, scrambled up the other side and sniffed the air, sensing his adversary immediately.

Recognizing the terrain from the other night, he followed the scent. The three-walled canyon wasn't far. Remembering how the jag had trapped him, he slowed his pace, moving cautiously. The closer he came to the canyon, the stronger the scent became, until he reached the top of the canyon where he raised himself on his haunches and sniffed. The powerful presence of the alien predator filled his senses, making his fur bristle.

A ringing sound pierced his brain. He moaned and it rang again, jarring him. His perceptions grew hazy. He turned and bolted down the slope, his senses fading with each step, then he slipped and tumbled, losing all sense of direction.

The ringing came again, jerking him back to his sleeping body. His eyes snapped open. His heart hammered against his ribs. His cell phone rang again. Stumbling out of the cot he snatched it up, his breath coming hard.

"Erik!" Nicole's voice, choked and full of terror. He heard a crash and a low growl. "Help!"

"What's the matter?" Another crash.

"A wild dog came through my window!"

He heard an angry growl that sent a nauseating chill skittering across his scalp.

"It's coming after me…"

Something crashed and the line went dead.

CHAPTER FORTY THREE

Erik raced up I-5 whipping in and out of traffic, white-knuckled hands clutching the wheel. His stomach felt as if a giant claw ripped at it. Every nerve and muscle in his body sang with tension. A group of cars bunched together ahead. He cut into the breakdown lane and passed them, pressing his foot to the floor as he pulled back toward the center of the road.

He ran the stop sign at the end of the exit ramp and slid sideways through the intersection, barely missing a station wagon. Two minutes later he turned the corner onto Nicole's street.

Flashing red, blue, and yellow lights filled the night.

An icy ball dropped into the pit of his stomach. He took a deep, jagged breath and roared down the street, skidding to a stop behind two squad cars. Bolting up the stairs to her apartment, he ran through the front door, startling a cop who spun toward him, hand on his gun. Erik plowed into him, knocking him to the floor before he could unholster his weapon.

Erik scrambled to his feet and took in the disarray. Nicole's coffee table lay turned on its side. Flowers lay crushed and trampled on the floor amid pieces of a broken vase. He heard noises from her bedroom and started toward it.

"Freeze!" the voice behind him said. He ignored it, heard a click and ducked into Nicole's bedroom.

Blood covered her carpet and bed. He stumbled from the force of the giddy feeling that flushed through him. Someone grabbed his arm. He shook his head. A nametag came into focus. ANDERSON. He looked into the face of a burly older cop with a bushy mustache. The young cop he had knocked down burst into the room, gun drawn, legs apart in a shooting stance.

"I've got him covered," he said.

"Put that fucking thing away, you asshole!" Anderson said. "This guy ain't going nowhere."

Erik forced himself to look back toward the bed. Nicole sat hunched against the headboard clutching a bloody phone, a dazed look in her eyes, arms covered with scratches and bites. Streaks of blood dried on her face. A dead Pit Bull lay sprawled in front of her on the bed amidst shards of a broken ceramic lamp, its fur matted dark black.

"Nicole!" Erik's voice shook. Hot tears came to his eyes.

She looked up at him blinking as if waking from a dream. "Erik?" she whispered.

Anderson let him go and he stumbled toward her. "Nicole!" he cried, choking. "Nicole." His heart rose in his throat. He climbed onto the bed and took her in his arms. She dropped the phone and clung to him, trembling as she whispered his name over and over again.

"That's a hell of a woman you got there," Anderson said. "One of the neighbors called, said she heard screams and a snarling dog. Apparently it got in through the window and attacked her." He nodded toward the Pit Bull's limp body. "Looks like she got a clean shot with the lamp."

The younger cop stepped forward brandishing handcuffs. "I'm placing you under arrest for assaulting a police officer."

Anderson held out his arm and blocked the younger man. "Get the fuck out of here and do something useful, Bennett."

"But he…"

"Came up here in a hurry, worried shitless about his girlfriend. Cut the Rambo shit and get your ass down to the cruiser to call in."

Bennett glared at Erik, then stormed out of the room. Anderson winked after he left. "Don't worry about Bennett. He's seen too many movies. You want me to call an ambulance?"

Erik looked at Nicole, who shook her head. "No thanks," he said. "I'll take her to emergency. I appreciate everything you've done. I didn't mean to…"

Anderson held up his hand. "Don't worry about it. He was overdue to be put in his place. You did me a favor. Saved me from having to do it. I'll put in a call to the animal removal squad to come get the dog," he said. "And if you don't mind, I'll wait here and lock up after they've gone. You better get your lady to a doctor. The dog might've been rabid, acting the way it did."

"You're right." Erik helped Nicole up from the bed and fumbled for a business card. "If you have any problems or questions, give me a call."

The cop took the card and studied it. "San Diego Zoo, huh?"

"You got any kids?"

"Two."

"When you get some time off give me a call. I'll get you and your family a behind-the-scenes V.I.P. tour."

"Yeah? Thanks, Mr. Simpson. I'll do that."

Erik took Nicole to Scripps Hospital for treatment. Her wounds were superficial, but they gave her a tetanus shot and treated her for shock to be safe.

An hour after calling Fritz, Erik walked toward his zoo office with his arm around Nicole, filling her in on the details of his discoveries. She listened, resting her head on his shoulder. Her resiliency in getting past the shock of the dog's attack impressed him.

"You want to talk about it?" he said softly.

She started shaking. "I'm not ready to talk yet," she said, squeezing his arm. "That dog scared the hell out of me, but I can't help thinking that it's not me that's in danger. It's you."

Erik didn't want to lie, but he was the one person who could stop Namaku and he would do what he had to. He stopped outside the door and turned to face her. "I don't know what I'd do if anything happened to you. Your safety comes first. Whether you like it or not you're going to spend the next few days with Fritz."

"Fritz?"

They heard footsteps and Fritz appeared from behind the building carrying a chimp. "Ah, Erik. Nicole. I'll be with you in a minute. It seems this little fellow got out of his cage. I found him running around out back."

"We'll meet you inside." Nicole yanked on Erik's sleeve. "I'll be safe with you," she whispered. "Let me stay."

Fritz waved and headed toward the compound. Erik and Nicole went to the office.

"I need to know you're safe so I can think straight," Erik whispered. "I have a score to settle with a jaguar."

Nicole frowned and opened her mouth, but Fritz reappeared before she could say anything.

Erik told him about the dog and asked him to watch Nicole while he searched for Namaku and the jaguar.

"Perhaps it would be better if I took her out of town for a day or two," Fritz said in a low voice.

"Good idea."

"I'm sure Ursula would love to have you," Fritz said turning to Nicole. "It's been lonely since the children moved away. Let me give her a call to tell her we're coming."

While Fritz called his wife, Nicole tried one last time to talk Erik into letting her stay.

Ten minutes later she left with Fritz.

Erik sat on the edge of the cot slamming his fist into his palm, trying to figure out his next move.

I've had enough of your shit, Namaku, he thought. You've robbed me of everyone I've loved. Until now. You're a vicious son-of-a-bitch and there's only one way to stop you. Laying back on the cot he closed his eyes and thought things through.

He came after Nicole tonight. That means he's on the move. If he is, if Namaku was down here raising hell, who's with the jag? It's been a long time since I've gone to it with my own free will. Every time I went to it, it was because Namaku wanted me there. What would happen if I go there myself?

Rising from the cot, he went out to his car and went through the camping gear in his trunk until he found the last of the plants he'd prepared up on Tahquitz peak. The mixture had dried and become hard, black, and gummy. After diluting it with water, he drank, gagging on the bitter liquid, then he lay back on the cot, closed his eyes and focused his thoughts on the jaguar.

Nausea came and passed until he saw familiar swirling geometric patterns in a smoky blue haze that grew in intensity until the door of light opened. A breeze came and lifted him, carrying him across the sky in a flash...

He found himself in a darkened cave. The first shadows of the approaching day illuminated the entrance with silvery-gray streaks of feeble light. A dark form huddled in front of him. Human. A low growl off to his right made him peer into the blackness. Two green orbs glittered like emeralds in the dark recesses of the cave.

Edging closer, he saw that a makeshift cage had been built into the back of the cave. The jaguar crouched, its eyes intent on his every move. Erik slipped through the wooden bars and faced the cat. His fear rose, but his anger held him immobile. The jag hunkered lower, then leaped. Erik let it pounce and in the next instant blackness swallowed him.

After a moment's disorientation, his senses cleared, then sharpened. What had been shadowy forms now came to him clearly. His legs felt strong and powerful, his smell keen.

He had become the jaguar.

He moved to the front of the cage, found the door and pawed the simple latch, letting himself out. In front of him lay the sleeping body of his brother, Namaku. He started toward him and stopped, his ears and nose poised toward the cave entrance. The sounds and smells of more humans came to him.

The National Guard, he thought. Didn't realize they'd come so close.

Namaku stirred. Erik lowered himself and crept forward until his head came within inches of his brother's face. It looked the same as he remembered, only fuller and more mature. Namaku looked peaceful at rest and for a moment Erik felt sorry for him.

He knew what he had to do, but now that he faced the reality he couldn't follow through. He thought of his two fathers, Phineas and Namsaui, then of Mitchell and the attack on Nicole. His rage kindled and merged with the instincts of the jaguar, but the urge to kill wasn't part of it. He could give himself over to the cat's savage urges, but his human nature held back as if keeping the lid on a boiling pot.

Namaku's eyes popped open, shocking Erik. In the next instant his brother was on him. Pain shot through him as Namaku plunged a knife into his shoulder. The cat's survival instincts erupted, stunning Erik's rational processes. Namaku stabbed again and the cat's rage took over.

They smashed against the cave wall and rolled across the floor toward the entrance, claws, teeth, and knife flashing in the dim light; two animals intent on destroying each other. Erik's claws raked his brother's back as the knife bit into his shoulder again. His jaws found the soft meat of Namaku's throat. They rolled out of the cave in a death embrace and tumbled down the side of a hill. Hot blood filled Erik's throat. His brother's gurgling cries filled his ear.

Startled voices greeted them from somewhere in the background.

"There he is! Killing a man!"

The sound of dozens of guns chambering rounds rang in Erik's ears. Namaku went limp. He could still hear the gurgling when he jumped away from the body. Shots pierced the morning air, biting into his flanks and neck. He took two steps and stumbled, all feeling leaving his rear legs. He pulled himself a few more yards, felt more white hot flashes of pain, then a popping sound and blackness.

CHAPTER FORTY FOUR

Though still in darkness, Erik knew by the warmth and sense of protection that he flew with the eagle. The pulse of its mighty wings filled him like the beating heart of a mother soothing an infant. The pain of the knife and bullet wounds had gone.

He became aware of several presences, each so distinct he felt he could reach out and embrace each one. Mitchell, his real mother and father, Phineas, and above them all Namsaui, as if he were their guide. Erik's heart swelled with both joy and loss. He wanted to go with them. *Be* with them.

He reached out with his heart and gave himself up; a smaller celestial body coming under the influence of a larger one. He drew closer, stopping as if a giant hand held him back.

No! the voice in his mind said. *It is not time.*

A great sadness pressed down on him. "I don't understand. I love all of you."

It is not right for us to take you so soon. You are needed.

Confusion engulfed him and the blackness faded into a swirling mist. Nicole's face swam into view. His heart went to her and he understood.

The mists came again, clearing to reveal the eagle. Erik became aware of its flapping wings and realized that it carried him. He looked up into its benevolent gaze.

The danger has not passed. You must finish what has begun and restore the balance. You are the chosen one. The one who wears the amulet. The keeper of the vision.

The eagle let go, sending Erik hurtling through the air the way he had when the vision began. His senses blurred and his mind lost focus.

He had a vague sense of drifting back into his body, feeling his breathing first, then his arms, torso, and legs. Something moved down by his foot before a light pressure slid up over it. Slithering. He opened his eyes and saw the blurry outline of a cobra work its way up his leg toward his head. He willed himself to move, but his body remained immobile, the combination of fear and drugs constricting his chest.

He remembered the cage he had put in his office earlier. Closing his eyes he focused his thoughts. The snake slid onto his torso, its presence creating a maddening distraction. Erik half-prayed, half-concentrated and willed himself back out of his body.

The snake moved onto his chest.

He felt it coil as darkness flooded in and he came back into consciousness in the body of his friend, the mongoose. Frantically, he nosed open the cage door and crossed the room in three leaps. The snake coiled on top of his human form, hooded head reared, poised to strike.

Erik bounded up onto the cot and the startled cobra swiveled to face him, emitting a stream of venom. Erik twisted to the side and dodged. Namaku's defiant eyes bore into him like twin fangs. Erik crouched and scrutinized the angry gaze that he knew so well, trying to fathom what lay behind it, sensing only hate. His fur bristled and stood erect as he prepared to fight his brother to the death.

Namaku raised higher still, head inching backward, mouth wide, rearing to strike. Erik jumped inside his attack and Namaku lunged. Erik twisted and the cobra's head bounced off his side, its fangs hitting his fur, away from his skin.

When Namaku reared to strike again, Erik darted to the side and caught the snake's head in his jaw. The cobra writhed, knocking him off his feet. He held tight while Namaku wrapped his coils around him and squeezed. Erik bit down harder and the snake thrashed back and forth slapping him from side to side. Erik sank his teeth deeper into the leathery head of his opponent as they rolled onto the floor.

His perceptions dimmed. Panic coursed through him. He held tight and thought he felt Namaku weaken until his awareness slipped and he lost consciousness...

...awakening in his human form. He sat up in time to see the cobra's tail twitch in its death throes. The mongoose released its grip on the snake's head and slid from between its lifeless coils. Sitting up on its haunches, the mongoose's eyes met Erik's. At that moment the first beam of morning sunlight came through the window, highlighting the little creature like a star performer in a circus.

Erik felt a surge of gratitude and the mongoose's fierce little eyes softened. It leaped onto the bed and curled up in his lap. Physically and emotionally spent, Erik held it close, patting it while studying the lifeless cobra on the floor.

The phone rang, startling both of them. Erik calmed his little friend and put him back in his cage. Moving in a daze, he picked up his cell phone.

"Hello?"

"Excuse me for calling so early, but I'm trying to reach Erik Simpson."

Erik recognized Captain Obeso's voice and knew the reason for the call. For once it didn't send him into an emotional maelstrom.

"We got the jag," Obeso said. "Near the canyon where you led us to the bear." His voice lowered. "We weren't in time to stop it from killing one more person, but we got it."

"Who's the victim?" Erik said, curious to hear how Namaku had come to the states.

"The guy's dressed as a ranger. Looks like he could be Indian or Spanish, but he has no I.D.. Schmitten's been running his fingerprints and description through the FBI files, Homeland Security, the INS, CIA, Interpol, you name it. He's coming up blank. It's like the guy dropped out of the sky or something. Schmitten wants to know if you'll come up and give a final, positive I.D. on the cat, maybe give us some idea of where it came from. He seems to think there might be a connection between the cat and this dead guy."

"I'll be there as soon as possible."

"Chopper's on the way."

"Somehow I knew you were going to say that."

They laughed, relieving a long standing tension. Erik enjoyed it. The first laugh he and Obeso ever shared and the first genuine laugh he'd had in a long time.

Erik studied the lifeless features of his brother, seeing the striking resemblance to Namsaui. A twinge of sadness shot through him when he thought of Phineas and Mitchell. He nodded and turned away as a National Guardsman rezipped the body bag.

He went back to the jaguar and examined the bullet riddled body, feeling sadness toward it, because he knew that it too had been his brother. A misused pawn in the hands of a jealous boy who could not understand that his father had loved him equally, if not more than his adopted son.

An angry snarl from one of the tracking dogs broke his reverie. He turned and his eyes met those of one of the dogs. For a moment he imagined that he saw the angry, defiant stare of his brother.

EPILOGUE

D r. Gilbert sat on his couch dozing in front of the television, his botany texts and notes scattered about him. On top of his papers sat a report from the Swedish government; the biographies of Erik's biological parents, a family picture and a copy of Erik's birth certificate. His cat Max stared at the open report, then jumped up on Gilbert's lap. The doctor opened his eyes and smiled. Max climbed up on his chest and tapped him on the side of the face with his paw.

The Old man frowned and patted the cat. "What's gotten into you Max? You've never acted like this before." The cat jumped down to the floor and bit at his pant leg, pulling at him like a playful puppy. "Max! What the hell are you doing?" The cat stood on its hind legs and pawed at the air, looking remarkably like a child beckoning for attention, then it leaped up onto the table and grabbed a sheet of paper with its mouth.

Gilbert watched dumb-founded as his cat took a pencil stub between its teeth and moved his head back and forth, scrawling squiggly lines on the paper. Gilbert rose from the couch and studied it, his eyes growing wide.

"I don't believe it," he whispered.

Leaning forward for a closer look he saw that the squiggly lines were letters that spelled out a message:

HI DOC. I PROMISED I'D EXPLAIN.

Max turned back to him, the pencil still in his mouth. Gilbert stared, unable to speak, unable to move. Max winked and resumed his scrawling.

WHAT'S THE MATTER, DOC? CAT GOT YOUR TONGUE?

ABOUT THE AUTHOR

Matthew J. Pallamary's historical novel of first contact between shamans and Jesuits in 18th century South America, titled, *Land Without Evil*, was published in hard cover by Charles Publishing, and has received rave reviews along with a San Diego Book Award for mainstream fiction. It was chosen as a Reading Group Choices selection. *Land Without Evil* was also adapted into a full-length stage and sky show, co-written by Agent Red with Matt Pallamary, directed by Agent Red, and performed by Sky Candy, an Austin Texas aerial group. The making of the show was the subject of a PBS series, Arts in Context episode, which garnered an EMMY nomination. *Land Without Evil* is in development as a feature film.

His nonfiction book, *The Infinity Zone: A Transcendent Approach to Peak Performance* is a collaboration with professional tennis coach Paul Mayberry which offers a fascinating exploration of the phenomenon that occurs at the nexus of perfect form and motion, bringing balance, power, and coordination to physical and mental activities. *The Infinity Zone* took 1st place in the International Book Awards, Nonfiction, New Age category, and was a finalist in the San Diego Book Awards

His first book, a short story collection titled *The Small Dark Room Of The Soul* was noted in The Year's Best Horror and Fantasy.

It's follow up *A Short Walk to the Other Side* was an International Book Award Finalist.

Dreamland, a novel about computer generated dreaming, written with Ken Reeth won an Independent e-Book Award in the Horror/Thriller category.

Matt's work has appeared in Oui, New Dimensions, The Iconoclast, Starbright, Infinity, Passport, The Short Story Digest, Redcat, The San Diego Writer's Monthly, Connotations, Phantasm, Essentially You, The Haven Journal, and many others. His fiction has been featured in The San Diego Union Tribune which he has also reviewed books for, and his work has been heard on KPBS-FM in San Diego, KUCI FM in Irvine, KX 93.5 in Laguna Beach, television Channel Three in Santa Barbara, and The Susan Cameron Block Show in Vancouver.

He has been a guest on the following nationally syndicated talk shows; Paul Rodriguez, In The Light with Michelle Whitedove, Susun Weed, Medicine Woman, Inner Journey with Greg Friedman, and Environmental Directions Radio series. Matt has also appeared on the following television shows; Bridging Heaven and Earth, Elyssa's Raw and Wild Food Show, Things That Matter, Literary Gumbo, Indie Authors TV, and ECONEWS. He has also been a frequent guest on numerous podcasts, among them, The Psychedelic Salon, and C-Realm.

He has taught fiction workshops at the Southern California Writers' Conference in San Diego, Palm Springs, and Los Angeles, and at the Santa Barbara Writers' Conference for twenty five years. He has also lectured at the Greater Los Angeles Writer's Conference, the Getting It Write conference in Oregon, the Saddleback Writers' Conference, the Rio Grande Writers' Seminar, the National Council of Teachers of English, The San Diego Writer's and Editor's Guild, The San Diego Book Publicists, The Pacific Institute for Professional Writing, and he has been a panelist at the World Fantasy Convention, Con-Dor, and Coppercon. He is presently Editor in Chief of Muse Harbor Publishing.

Matt also received the Man of the Year 2000 from San Diego Writer's Monthly Magazine. His memoir *Spirit Matters*, which details his journeys to Peru, working with shamanic plant medicines took first place in the San Diego Book Awards Spiritual Book Category, and was an Award-Winning Finalist in the autobiography/memoir category of the National Best Book Awards, sponsored by USA Book News. *Spirit Matters* is also available as an audio book.

Matt frequently visits the jungles, mountains, and deserts of North, Central, and South America pursuing his studies of shamanism and ancient cultures.

WWW.MATTPALLAMARY.COM

BOOKS BY MATTHEW J. PALLAMARY

THE SMALL DARK ROOM OF THE SOUL

LAND WITHOUT EVIL

SPIRIT MATTERS

DREAMLAND (WITH KEN REETH)

THE INFINITY ZONE (WITH PAUL MAYBERRY)

A SHORT WALK TO THE OTHER SIDE

CYBERCHRIST

NIGHT WHISPERS

www.ingramcontent.com/pod-product-compliance
Lightning Source LLC
Chambersburg PA
CBHW070124260626
47160CB00004B/1608